"Why did [...] **Her voice** held a hint of temper.

This reaction he recognized. This he could handle. His own body stirred in response, but he didn't allow his attention to stray to her lush lips, which begged to be kissed, nor did he let himself tangle his fingers in her silky hair. "Should I not follow my runaway fiancée?"

She swallowed and raised an eyebrow. "Are we engaged? I guess I must have missed the moment I said yes, among all the fanfare of your proposal."

"Something did not meet your satisfaction," he continued. "Maybe you were still hoping for a fairy-tale marriage?"

Her cheeks flushed, and he could see he was on the right track.

"You have nothing to worry about," she said, and the corners of her mouth turned down. "I have no illusions of a happy ending between us."

"There will be plenty of happy endings between us, Cara," he said, letting his voice turn rough with the fire that blazed through him at these words. "That is a promise. But I am a far cry from Prince Charming. As you might have noted."

A sizzling new duet from Harlequin Presents debut author Rebecca Hunter!

The Carandini Legacy

Double the brothers...means twice the trouble!

Italian tycoons Massimo and Alessandro have climbed the downward spiral of their scandalous parents' empire. It took blood, sweat and tears to redeem the Carandini name. Finally, the twin brothers have the world in their hands. But now comes their biggest challenge yet, and there's a lot more than just their empire at stake...

Massimo Carandini is cool, calm and collected. His carefully selected fiancée, Catarina d'Avalos, will consolidate the stability of his business. But when Catarina refuses to be neatly filed away in her own marriage and flees, Massimo must track her down and convince her to return as his bride!

Read Massimo and Catarina's story in
Convenient Wife Conditions
Available now!

And don't miss Alessandro and Ann-Sophie's story in
Heir to Italian Altar
Coming soon!

CONVENIENT WIFE CONDITIONS

REBECCA HUNTER

PRESENTS

If you purchased this book without a cover you should be aware that this book is stolen property. It was reported as "unsold and destroyed" to the publisher, and neither the author nor the publisher has received any payment for this "stripped book."

Recycling programs for this product may not exist in your area.

ISBN-13: 978-1-335-21372-3

Convenient Wife Conditions

Copyright © 2026 by Rebecca Hunter

All rights reserved. No part of this book may be used or reproduced in any manner whatsoever without written permission.

Without limiting the exclusive rights of any author, contributor or the publisher of this publication, any unauthorized use of this publication to train generative artificial intelligence (AI) technologies is expressly prohibited. Harlequin also exercises their rights under Article 4(3) of the Digital Single Market Directive 2019/790 and expressly reserves this publication from the text and data mining exception.

This is a work of fiction. Names, characters, places and incidents are either the product of the author's imagination or are used fictitiously. Any resemblance to actual persons, living or dead, businesses, companies, events or locales is entirely coincidental.

For questions and comments about the quality of this book, please contact us at CustomerService@Harlequin.com.

TM and ® are trademarks of Harlequin Enterprises ULC.

 Harlequin Enterprises ULC
22 Adelaide St. West, 41st Floor
Toronto, Ontario M5H 4E3, Canada
www.Harlequin.com

HarperCollins Publishers
Macken House, 39/40 Mayor Street Upper,
Dublin 1, D01 C9W8, Ireland
www.HarperCollins.com

Printed in Lithuania

Rebecca Hunter is an award-winning author, reader, traveler, occasional college professor, full-time chocolate lover and keeper of a very messy desk. Her books have won the National Excellence in Romance Fiction Award (NERFA), the HOLT Medallion and the Vivian Award. She writes witty, passionate stories about complex characters and intriguing destinations for the Harlequin Presents line. For reading and writing updates, photos and travel plans, join her newsletter on her website: www.rebeccahunterwriter.com.

This is Rebecca Hunter's debut book
for Harlequin Presents—we hope that you enjoy it!

Visit the Author Profile page at Harlequin.com.

To the best author crew—Addie, Adrianne, Amy, Anne, Dafina, Elizabeth, Jackie, Kilby, Ro and Shannon—for all your love and support on my path to Harlequin Presents. SBC forever!

CHAPTER ONE

"The wedding will be scheduled for two months from now," said Giuseppe d'Avalos, third-generation head of his family's far-reaching empire. "That is the soonest it can take place without suggesting more urgent reasons for this marriage."

Massimo Carandini took a drink of his grappa to hide his scowl at the hint of scandal suggested in the man's words. He swallowed, letting the liquid run a warm trail down his throat, then leaned back in the leather armchair and gave d'Avalos a tight smile. "Agreed. And I will defer to your daughter on the location and details of the event."

Massimo glanced toward one of the library's window seats, where Catarina d'Avalos quietly listened to the conversation. She was angled toward her father, so all he could make out was a long tangle of chestnut tresses, white trousers and a satin top the color of the sea. He thought he saw her nod, an acknowledgment that she was in agreement with their plan, but the bursts of sunlight filtering through the yellows, oranges and reds of the tall stained-glass window made it difficult to be sure.

The window lit the room, casting a warm glow on

brass lamps, rows of old books and museum-quality relics of the past. Arched alcoves lined the interior walls, featuring old portraits of self-important men and women, undoubtedly evidence of the family's pedigree. If the property itself wasn't enough. This was the kind of estate that marked the legacy Massimo Carandini's grandfather had sacrificed his life for. And then his father had squandered it.

An engagement was the last thing Massimo wanted to waste business hours on this afternoon. And yet, here he was, missing a key meeting to spend an hour in the library of this sprawling home, just to close this deal with Catarina d'Avalos. Because the desire to restore his family's name once and for all far outweighed his distaste for marriage.

Massimo's aversion to this arrangement was not personal. His future bride was lovely by all accounts. Before he had approached Giuseppe d'Avalos with his offer, Massimo's assistant had provided him with photos, one from a fundraiser, where she wore a rich red gown and a demure smile, her glossy brown hair swept into some sort of twist at the base of her long neck. Another showed Catarina alongside her parents after the opening night of one of her mother's performances. She was attractive, if not beautiful. Massimo supposed it would be helpful to find his fiancée attractive, even if it wasn't his primary concern.

He had studied and then dismissed two other equally attractive but less suitable potential candidates. The first, minor nobility, had a well-polished image by day that belied her preference for much wilder nights. The second he'd rejected when his assistant had discovered the topless photos someone had taken of her at a party. He didn't condemn a taste for wild nights or topless photos on principle, but his own purposes were very specific. If it had only taken a few strokes of the keyboard to dig up those pieces of evidence, what would the paparazzi uncover when their marriage came under closer scrutiny? Massimo wasn't interested in finding out.

Giuseppe d'Avalos must have also seen his daughter's nod or somehow gotten the response he was looking for because he returned his attention back to Massimo.

"Yours is not the first offer of marriage that a business associate has proposed," the man said.

Massimo didn't mistake his casual tone for anything that neared offhandedness.

"I have no doubt," he murmured. There was an empire behind her, generations of money and acquisitions, and as the only child, it would all fall to Catarina.

"But yours is the first I have seriously considered," the man continued. "You have a reputation for following through on your commitments, despite…"

D'Avalos waved his hand through the air dismissively, as if it was unnecessary to detail the train wreck of Massimo's father's business failures. As if the whole world knew enough about the rise and fall of the Carandini family legacy that he didn't have to put it into words.

Massimo gritted his teeth, resisting every steely retort that came to mind. How long would the sins of his father be used as a lens to analyze every decision he made? Hadn't he shown that he was not the kind of man who would, for example, spend investors' money on a "company" yacht simply because his wife demanded it? But this was a business deal, like any other, he reminded himself. Except, in this case, he couldn't leave the velvet-cloaked negotiations to his brother. He had to deal with this one himself.

"Trust is the foundation of this deal on both sides," he said smoothly, as if references to the disgrace that marked his father's legacy simply rolled off him.

The marriage would secure the future of both the families' businesses, but most importantly, a stable, appropriate marriage would prove to the world that the scandals that had plagued the Carandini family were firmly in the past. No more wary investor meetings; no more whispers about that one terrible night on the yacht. So while he wanted a wife who would be a suitable companion at high-profile events, he had instructed his assistant that his first priority was for the woman to have absolutely no controversy attached to her name. She should be a blank slate as far as the media was concerned so as to lend a stable, calming presence to the Carandini name. This was harder to find than one might think in the age of social media, where people regularly and willingly—*willingly*—offered documentation of their private lives for the world to see.

In this area, Massimo would not compromise. Truth be told, compromise never had much appeal, nor much use, in his life. Ever since coming of age, he and his twin brother, Alessandro, had worked single-mindedly to restore the family's fortunes and reputation, both of which his parents had so quickly and thoroughly ruined. Massimo and Alessandro had made it their lives' work to restore their grandfather's crumbling shipping empire that had fallen into ruins and make it bigger, better, grander than ever. None of their accomplishments were built on compromise.

However, public opinions were unpredictable, fickle and not nearly as controllable as the business itself had proven to be. So while their profits had increased, the stench of their parents' public drama still clung to the family name. It was holding them back.

After a lifetime of living with their parents' public fights, their preoccupation with each other at the expense of everything else, neither brother was interested in marriage. However, during one of many endless strategy meetings with PR firms and specialists, the solution became unavoidable: They needed to show the world that this generation of the Carandini family was not cut from the same cloth as the last. They needed to prove that a marriage—because everyone assumed the brothers would inevitably marry someday, no matter how often they discouraged this idea—would not result in the same downward spiral that had caught hold of their parents and never let them go.

Of course, Alessandro had argued that Massimo should be the one to go through with said marriage.

"How convenient for you," Massimo had responded in his driest tone. "Though I can't help but point out that you're far more suitable to find a wife than I am."

"If you're referencing my reputation for understanding what women enjoy, then yes," Alessandro had said in that lazy voice of his. He used it to close business deals as often as he used it to charm the women that seemed to flock to him.

"But we are discussing a marriage that will not spur hungry paparazzi to dig through their archives for old speculations to rekindle. A marriage that does not attract scandal," his brother had continued. "That is your territory."

Massimo had scowled at Alessandro, the way he always did when his brother was right. Alessandro's public reputation was only saved by his carefree facade. He had all but publicly declared his permanent playboy status, and women knew this when they entered into anything that could be mistaken for an entanglement. His brother's image wouldn't work for a marriage that inherently implied stability. Massimo, on the other hand, had no qualms about showing himself as the relentlessly calculating businessman that he was. His public persona quite accurately aligned with the relationship he expected: a marriage free of the illusion of love, strictly for convenience.

"I'm already doing my part to sway public opinion in our family's favour, one woman at a time," Alessandro had added with a smirk. "You, on the other hand, are determined to force your iron will onto the rest of the world. If anyone is in the position to change our family's reputation, it's you."

He said all of this with a lazy, knowing drawl that got under Massimo's skin. Especially since, once again, his brother was right. If Massimo showed that his steely reputation would not be bent with marriage, that would certainly settle any lingering doubts that this generation of Carandinis would not make the same mistakes as the last.

D'Avalos looked in the direction of Catarina again, and Massimo sensed the man was gathering his words. He waited, observing his future father-in-law. D'Avalos was impeccably dressed in a well-tailored shirt and dark wool slacks. His hair was streaked with silver, and his brow creased with evidence of heavy sorrow and loss. The man had rarely smiled even before the untimely death of his wife, Marie Nordland, the so-called Nordic Siren, and now, *rarely* had swerved closer to *never*.

When d'Avalos looked back at Massimo, his gaze was almost wistful.

"I have never claimed to understand my daughter," he said in a low, serious voice. "However, Catarina's future is more important to me than anything else in this world."

D'Avalos's steely gaze flickered with hints of emotion, but just as quickly, all traces were gone.

"My wife's last wish was for me to make sure that Catarina is taken care of for as long as she lives," he continued. "I have arranged this marriage for her because I am not a young man. Catarina was a surprise and a blessing to both my wife and me. I recognize I will not always be here to carry out my promise, so I would be trusting that to you."

"Your trust would not be misplaced," Massimo replied.

Though there were plenty of things this marriage

would not be, providing for Catarina was straightforward. She would have his money, and his residences, plane, cars and boats would be at her disposal. She would be able to live the lifestyle she was accustomed to. Massimo wasn't sure what d'Avalos saw on his face, but it seemed to satisfy him. The man stood and turned once again to his daughter.

"Catarina," said d'Avalos in a voice that was both gruff and tender, as if, even after twenty-four years, he still was not quite sure how to talk to his daughter. "I will leave you to make your final decision."

The older man retreated from the room, and the door closed with a quiet snick. Through the rays of light, Massimo thought he saw Catarina's back straighten. Her shoulders rose and fell, as if she was fortifying herself with a deep breath. He felt a stab of sympathy for this woman, whose future was determined in backroom business deals. Then she lifted her chin, stood and turned to him.

Massimo couldn't explain what came next, except that she met his gaze and something happened. Something *must* have happened, he would later tell himself, because he was unaware of anything else except the feeling that the entire world had suddenly stopped. All he could do was drink this woman in. Her eyes were a shade darker than her chestnut hair, and they were wide, curious, with an openness he had no idea what to do with.

Her lips parted slightly. They were full and pouty, as if they were made for pleasure. And then he was thinking about pleasure in detail. Hers. His. An electric jolt of desire ran through him, shaking him out of this strange stupor. Massimo blinked, and much to his dismay, he found that he was standing, too, though he had no memory of rising to his feet. He gritted his teeth and shoved all thoughts of pleasure to the dark recesses of his mind.

Massimo knew how to handle attraction, satisfyingly for both parties and without any lingering sentiment. That was exactly how their marriage would be conducted. He wasn't the kind of man who had time for wants and needs, not his nor anyone else's. Clear expectations should be set from the beginning. But first, she needed to agree to this marriage.

"It's a pleasure to meet you," he said, giving her a charming smile. Charm was a skill like any other, something that he had mastered with ruthless efficiency and exercised when necessary. Most often it wasn't necessary, he had found. Today was an exception, he told himself.

"The pleasure is mine."

He hadn't fully understood Marie Nordland's moniker, the Nordic Siren, until this moment. Without a doubt, the famous soprano had passed her voice down to her daughter. Massimo was sure of it because Catarina's voice floated inside him, light and beautiful and somehow pushing away all other thought. It hummed in him, filling his senses with a song that could bring a man to his knees. Here, in the quiet, subdued library, filled with dark shelves and leather-bound books, her voice rang like a bell, echoing through his well-tempered senses. Massimo steeled himself against the rush of pleasure the soft music of her words conjured. It was no wonder that

Giuseppe d'Avalos kept his daughter practically locked up in this estate. How many men would be pounding on the door if they heard her voice? The thought was an ugly thing that he shoved somewhere deep inside.

"You must have been told many times that you have your mother's voice," he commented, keeping his own voice mild.

She gave him a hint of a smile. "But not my mother's taste for the stage. To my parents' eternal disappointment."

Her tone was so light, so airy, as if ignoring family expectations could be brushed off. A sudden wave of resentment washed over him, the resentment for the position his parents had put his brother and him in, the duty the brothers were bound to. What a privileged life Catarina had lived that she could simply choose not to follow her family's wishes because they didn't suit her. And still, her father was looking after her, smoothing out her future. She had been protected. Coddled, even. But the usual resentment bubbling inside him was overshadowed by something else, something darker. He pushed aside this strange feeling in his gut.

These privileges were the very qualities that made her a perfect wife for him, he reminded himself. She was not hungry for attention, for money, for the temptations that a life as his wife might present. She could rise above whatever they faced. He couldn't forget that he was closing a business deal, like any other. So Massimo quashed the last of his simmering bitterness and focused on the woman in front of him.

As Catarina walked toward him, Massimo couldn't

ignore the grace with which she moved. Her brown hair spread out in waves over her shoulder, and her azure blouse moved like the placid waters of the Mediterranean. He could see why her mother had insisted on her being cared for in her dying wish. There was something ethereal, something otherworldly, about her. She was lovely, a perfect choice, he told himself, ignoring the faint warning bells ringing deep inside him.

He watched her as she seemed to glide across the room, taking slow steps, her eyes focused on him. Her expression wasn't deliberately seductive, the way countless women approached him when they wanted some combination of sex, power or money from him. Instead, it was as if she held a secret, one just for him. The warning bells rang louder.

"It's a strange thing, meeting the man my father has arranged for me to marry," she said softly. There was that openness in her gaze again, a curiosity.

Massimo gave her a smile, calculated to put her at ease, resisting the sizzle of attraction that grew hotter with each of her steps. He could do this, he told himself. He was in control of his emotions. He wasn't his father. "I hope I meet your expectations."

"Of course," she said, and her lovely cheeks turned a golden red. "My father will always look out for my best interests."

He thought he detected a hint of wryness in her voice, but her placid smile simply suggested contentment.

Catarina came to a stop in front of him, close enough that he was tempted to brush his hand against her cheek, just to test the softness of her skin. He found himself studying her dark eyes, those long lashes. The electric pull took hold of him again, and something white-hot arched between them as she rose onto her tiptoes. Her scent was everywhere, roses and the salty kiss of the sea, swirling around him. She brushed her lips against one cheek, then the other.

It was an everyday greeting, nothing more, but Massimo felt as if something echoed between them, reverberating deep inside him, something strange and new. It was as if the brush of her lips on his skin called to the deepest, most hidden part inside him. And he *wanted*. He wanted badly. That part of him roared to life, the part he had spent every day of his adult life burying, beating into submission. *Give in*, the siren's song called. It grew, expanding inside him, then exploded to life, roaring a single word: *mine*.

The word clanged through him like an alarm, its screech too loud to ignore. This was the force his father had given in to, the seductive pull that had dragged down Massimo and Alessandro in its wake. Never would he succumb to it. Massimo would never be his father. So he shoved all these feelings back down, deep inside him, once and for all.

CHAPTER TWO

CATARINA HAD SEEN Massimo before. It was in a lush ballroom somewhere in Milan, lit by sparkling chandeliers. She remembered a chocolate fountain, a black Steinway piano in a corner that she'd admired and an army of waitstaff, dressed in all black and buzzing around with bottles of champagne. She remembered the silk of her gown, blue and whisper-soft against her skin. She remembered the stylist's expert hands in her hair, testing one updo after another as her mother sat beside her, blue eyes warm and so very alive. Her mother had always been the sun of the family, lighting it up, and Catarina was content to be an outer planet, kept in close by gravity, deferring to larger planets as long as her mother's steady warmth and energy were near.

She remembered the hall with its red velvet curtains and the murmur of the crowd over the hum of the string quartet. And she remembered Massimo, at the center of it all. At least, he'd seemed to be the center to her at the time. Massimo Carandini didn't notice her, of course. At sixteen, she had been a shy, wide-eyed girl in a demure gown, all but hiding in the shadow of her mother's glowing presence.

But she'd noticed him. How could anyone not be drawn to this tall man with captivating brown eyes, a bespoke suit and silky black hair that she'd inexplicably wanted to touch. In a room full of men in elegant suits just like his, Massimo Carandini shouldn't have stood out, but he did. There was a hardness about him, something distant and forbidding that made her sixteen-year-old self feel things she hadn't recognized at the time. *What made someone hard like that?* she had wondered. Why was she struck by the strange desire to run her hand over the hard line of his jaw, the stark planes of his cheeks, searching for hints of softness?

But that was years ago, back when her life had been a series of questions, girlish and ultimately inconsequential. Would she rather attend an all-girls boarding school in England or in the Alps, closer to home? Would she rather spend the fall in Taipei learning Mandarin, or did she want to work for her mother? Back then, gaining freedom from her father's controlling hand hadn't crossed her mind, and her mother was still around to temper his tendency to turn concerns into rigid rules. So each time, she had chosen to stay closer to home. She had chosen with her heart, and now, in the devastating aftermath of her mother's death, she was grateful that she had. At sixteen, Catarina had known that the choices she had been given were privileges and that life was unfair that way, but her life simply *was*. She hadn't questioned it, much less considered how she would feel if her life were to upend, suddenly and irrevocably.

Now, every day, she lived with the bone-deep understanding of what the loss of her mother meant for her.

Catarina was alone. At first, she hadn't quite noticed the narrowing of her independence, or if she did, she attributed it to her loss, her solitude. It had taken a long time before she was aware of the way her father's worries had turned into restrictions.

Still, when her father came to her with a proposal for marriage, she hadn't contemplated any deeper questions, such as: Should her father even be involved in her plans for marriage? Catarina had focused instead on the freedom she would gain when she escaped her father's watchful gaze. When he'd floated the name Massimo Carandini specifically, she'd asked herself a second question: How had this man made her feel back in that ballroom when she was sixteen? He had made her shiver with what she now understood was desire. From across the room, no less. That feeling had been private, unattached from her famous mother. And it had felt like the opposite of being alone.

Then there was the fact that, despite his oppressive impulses, she trusted her father implicitly, so why wouldn't she comply with his wishes? Why wouldn't she do her best to make her father happy? She'd promised that much to her mother in her final days, that she would look after her father's happiness.

Now, in her favorite room of the house, surrounded by books that had buoyed her through darker times, Catarina stared at the stranger in front of her, reminding herself of all the rationales for this arrangement that had floated through her mind.

She thought she had prepared herself for the moment she'd face the object of her teenage crush, for the inevitable conclusion of her mother's last wish and her father's relentless determination to fulfil it. It was a decision that would bring to rest the uncertainty of the past few years since her mother's death. But nothing inside her was at ease. Instead, it was as if the hum of an electric current ran through her, unexpected and shockingly intimate.

As she gazed at the man in front of her, she could see she had made a grave miscalculation. Her father had always treated her as if he was a little baffled by her, like she was another species, a favorite dog, perhaps, content with pats on the head and endless treats. So although her best interests were always at the forefront of her father's mind, why had she assumed that Giuseppe d'Avalos would know who would make a good marriage partner for her? How could her father possibly know what she needed in a husband, what she could handle? Because the man in front of her was far too much to handle. Just the sensation of being close to Massimo threatened to overwhelm her.

Up close, it was clear that her memories didn't do justice to this man. His lean, muscular frame was starker than she remembered, more imposing, more *everything*. She could see the outline of the well-defined muscles of his shoulders under the crisp white of his shirt. The top button was undone, showing a hint of dusky hair against bare skin, so shockingly intimate, so sexual and not at all in line with the inscrutable expression on his face. That perfectly fitted shirt followed his broad chest, his tapered waist and disappeared into charcoal-gray wool pants.

Was she really focusing on this man's pants? Her gaze flicked back to his face as her cheeks flushed. She was not ready to identify all the feelings that were running through her. Instead, she met his eyes. But none of her memories captured the piercing intensity of his dark brown eyes as he watched her. They drew her in, pulling her toward him. She wanted to touch him. She wanted to test the softness of his inky hair between her fingers, the smooth line of his jaw. She inhaled, and his scent filled her, spicy, masculine with a hint of pine that sent her thoughts to her house deep in a remote Norwegian fjord. This was the scent of freedom, and she wanted more.

Catarina couldn't help herself. She lifted up onto her tiptoes and brought her lips to one cheek, pressing them against his soft skin. Just a greeting, she told herself as she took another breath of his scent. Nothing more. But her heart slammed in her chest, beating out its message, *liar, liar, liar.* Still, she moved to the other cheek, greedy for more. When her lips met his skin again, she heard the quietest of groans from somewhere deep inside him. It was electric. *Magical.* The word resonated inside her, as part of her battered heart opened up in what felt very much like hope.

Catarina was scared to move. She was scared to breathe. If she did, she might disturb this feeling inside her, the feeling that there was hope, that maybe she didn't have to spend the rest of her life alone. Maybe her mother wasn't the only person she would ever grow close to, who would understand her. Maybe this marriage wouldn't simply be a compromise she was forced to make, her father's satisfaction for fulfilling her mother's dying wish in exchange for the freedom of a life out from under her father's scrutiny, not dictated by his misguided maneuvers. Maybe this marriage could be more than a business arrangement. No one would ever replace her mother, and that was the last thing she wanted, but maybe there was a chance that Catarina had found another connection.

Then something shifted. Massimo's expression seemed to shutter, leaving only a distant stillness. She stared at the man in front of her, so remote, searching for the connection she had felt just moments before. It had to be there, somewhere inside him, because it was still bubbling inside her. It had been there before, and she would find it again.

Catarina could feel her determination grow. She had spent too much of her life buffeted by her mother's awful twist of fate, by her father's autocratic decisions. This man in front of her was an opening in her future. Clinging to that electric pull she'd felt, that groan of pleasure she swore she'd heard, she took a deep breath and squared her shoulders at this imposing man. *Just a man*, she reminded herself.

"Massimo?"

Just his name, nothing else, as she tried to capture into words the questions that reverberated inside her. *What is this overwhelming pull between us? Don't you feel what I feel right now?*

Massimo closed his eyes, his long, dark lashes resting on his cheeks, and she thought she detected a faint shudder or a grimace or some reaction that she couldn't read. Then, when he opened his eyes again, her blood ran cold as that last spark of hope, the one she was clinging to, drained from her body. In front of her was the man she had seen in photos, a self-contained, arrogant man with a coldness that was unmistakable. It was as if he had just turned off every emotion, so methodically and thoroughly, leaving absolutely no trace of the man whose cheeks she had brushed her lips against, the man whose eyes had flashed with desire and something else.

Or maybe he hadn't turned off his emotions. Maybe this was who Massimo Carandini really was, and what she had mistaken for a connection had been just a facade for her father's benefit that he'd let linger. Maybe this was the true face of the man underneath it. The man she would marry. Catarina swallowed.

"Miss d'Avalos." Her name rolled off his tongue, velvet-soft, both a caress and a warning.

"We are to be engaged," she said, pulling her thoughts in order. "Surely first names are appropriate."

He frowned, disapproval radiating from him.

"What I require of a wife is someone who will maintain an impeccable reputation," he said, his gaze fixed on her, impenetrable as the silky tone washed over her.

How could his voice leave her so aware of the way her shirt brushed over her breasts each time she breathed? Catarina tried to focus on the fact that he didn't seem to find her comment worthy of a response.

"I will require you to attend dinners where we will entertain business clients," he continued in a cool, imperious tone. "We will make regular public appearances to ensure that the world understands the stability of our partnership. Our priority is to portray the image of stability."

He enunciated that last word slowly, as if she might have missed all the implications of the values he was laying out. Catarina resisted a frown. She tried to read his face for some hint of emotion, but she found it impenetrable, a wall of stone. If this was the kind of interaction he wanted, she had a lifetime full of practice with it. Growing up with her mother in the spotlight, she had learned early never to show her emotions. Hopes, dreams and disappointments were saved for the privacy of her own home, for her family. That was the nature of having the Nordic Siren for a mother. Any hint of discontent would be picked apart by the paparazzi, each observation fueling a spiral of further interest and speculation. Catarina would never subject her family to that. But at home, away from crowds and prying eyes, she could finally exit the stage, and she had found relief in that freedom. How foolish she had been to so quickly slot Massimo into the role of family. The loss of the warmth of her family had been a gaping hole inside her since her mother's death, and she could not expect marriage to Massimo to fill it. Still, she needed to clarify the terms of this engagement.

Catarina kept her face serene, tilting her head to the side. "This proposal sounds an awful lot like a business negotiation."

His eyes grew even darker, more distant. "I was given to understand that you were clear about the nature of our agreement."

"I am," she said lightly, as if she wasn't negotiating her entire future. "I suppose I just wondered if there would be any ceremony to this, perhaps a ring or a proposal on one knee, just for tradition's sake."

She gave a little laugh, the kind that had amused and enchanted the crowds that her mother drew.

Massimo did not smile. "I kneel for no one."

"Noted," she said mildly.

His eyes narrowed as if he was searching for sarcasm, for any hint of rebellion. But he wouldn't find it. She had learned long ago, in her endless dealings with her father, that challenging a man like this directly was not the most effective strategy. Instead, she changed tactics.

"I will, of course, require time for study. I put off university to be by my mother's side." Catarina hadn't actually applied for university or even thoroughly considered this path, but it was one of many roads to freedom she had entertained before her father had dropped this marriage into her lap. Her comment was a test of sorts, she supposed, one that she had the uneasy feeling Massimo might fail. Too late, Catarina realized she should have asked for the results much earlier.

Massimo didn't react to the mention of her mother, let alone offer the condolences that usually followed any reference to their family's devastating loss. Instead, he waved a dismissive hand. "You can schedule that with my assistant to ensure it doesn't conflict with the functions we will attend."

Catarina smiled pleasantly at him as she digested his words, trying to ignore the heaviness that weighed in her gut. This man was as autocratic as her father, but a future with him would be much worse. Giuseppe d'Avalos loved her, and regardless of how ham-fisted his attempts to steer her life had been, she had never once doubted that his intentions were true. He only wanted the best for her.

But Massimo Carandini didn't care about her happiness. That much was clear. This man hadn't sworn on her mother's deathbed to take care of her. Instead, he was looking for an expensive, showy decoration, paid for with the kind of upscale exchanges that were made in a study filled with the scent of grappa and cigars. None of the fruits of those deals would come her way if she married this man. Massimo would treat her like a prop, brought out when he needed her and put away afterward. Catarina had been stuck in her father's gilded cage for the past two years, as they'd struggled to find a way forward in a world without her mother. But Massimo's cage would be much smaller, and he wasn't even pretending it would be gilded.

Catarina had told herself she would go through with this marriage for her father's sake, but staring at the cold, implacable man in front of her, she was no longer sure she could. And yet, she had to. Her father had rested the future of his business on this union. And no matter how different they were, she loved her father and wanted to please him. She wanted to allow him to rest easy. But how could she promise her life to a man like Massimo? There had to be a solution. It was just so hard to think rationally when he was so close. His body seemed to call to hers.

She smiled pleasantly at Massimo as he glared at her, and she found herself searching for a chink in his armor of demands and control. This was a man who didn't even think to downplay his arrogant commands on their first meeting, before she had even agreed to their marriage. Clearly, Massimo didn't have enough people in his life who said no to him.

"I do so look forward to our next meeting, but I am afraid I have business to attend to this morning," she said. "Unless you were expecting a romantic walk through our gardens first…"

She followed her delicate jab with a bland smile. A flash of surprise crossed his face, as if the last thing he'd expected was this poke at him followed by a dismissal. It disappeared immediately, but the glimmer of satisfaction inside her lasted longer.

"We will have plenty of time to talk about future expectations," he said, his low voice rich and ominous.

That voice slid through her, leaving her breasts heavy and heat pooling between her legs. This was what made him so dangerous. Her body didn't seem to care about cages, gilded or not, even if they belonged to closed-off men with iron wills. Despite everything he'd said, she still had the inexplicable urge to run her fingers over his full lips, so improbably sensual against the hard set of his jaw. Though she'd all but told him to leave, a part of her ached for him to protest, to close the distance between them and press her mouth against his lush lips. If just his cheeks were enough to spark heat inside her, what would his lips do to this feeling inside her?

But Massimo didn't kiss her. He just stared at her with that cold, assessing gaze, as if he was calculating her use to him. Then, without another word, he turned and walked out the door.

Catarina stood in place for a long time, in the middle of the library, the shelves of books glowing red and orange in the light from the windows. But she wasn't thinking about books. She was thinking of Massimo and those deep brown eyes that, for a few moments, had seemed to be a window into a more private part of him.

No. She must have imagined those few moments, imposing her own spin on the distinctly less charming reality of her life. It wouldn't be the first time. She'd spent enough of her childhood entertaining herself with her imagination to know how easily ideas could turn fantastical.

Later that evening at dinner, Catarina smiled pleasantly across the table through course after course as her father ticked off characteristics that made Massimo the perfect husband: money, family name—tarnished but redeemed—and multiple estates for her exploration. She didn't miss his unspoken assumption that this list should make her happy, and she didn't say a word, just murmured in assent and let her father talk.

As he continued his expounding, Catarina found herself thinking about her mother. How would her father's ideas about marriage have played out if Maria Nordland had lived? Even before her mother's death, her father's overprotective tendencies had been stifling at times. That he loved Catarina had never been in doubt, but he had never quite figured out what to do with her, swinging wildly between indulgent and strict. Her mother had protected her from her father's efforts to raise the society girl that he had always assumed someone of their station would become. In that path, Catarina had no interest. She had only sporadically attended the all-girls boarding school, tucked away in the Italian Alps, staying just long enough to learn languages and anything of interest before she took off to be by her mother's side for their next adventures. A flurry of tutors had ensured she'd passed all her exams, but many of the finishing school lessons this academy prided itself on were lost on Catarina. After eighteen, she had resisted her father's more pressing calls for an appropriate future and assumed the position of her mother's full-time travel companion. Her life might have glided on like that for years, but her mother's stage-four breast cancer diagnosis five years ago had changed everything.

From that day on, Catarina's life had been turned upside down. Her mother had been her only real friend, and when they traveled, it was as if the two of them had existed in their own little world. At the age when she might have entertained the idea of university or some small stretch of independence, she grew even more attached to her mother. At every single one of those last performances, she and her father had sat, side by side, in tears, bonded by their mutual love and impending loss. During those last months, the world had closed. It was then that her mother's last wishes were uttered, the wishes that had haunted both Catarina and her father since that day. She had eavesdropped outside the heavy door to her parents' bedroom, unwilling to miss a moment of what was left of her mother's voice.

"Protect her," her mother had said to her father. Her mother's voice had been so soft, so weak, so unlike the larger-than-life music that had shaped Catarina's world. "She will be lonely when I am gone. Make sure that she is protected for the rest of her life."

If Catarina hadn't eavesdropped that day, she never would have understood what was behind her father's clumsy attempts to push her in one direction, then the other. But when he announced the plan for her marriage across the heavy dinner table, surrounded by portraits of generations of the d'Avalos family, a rare smile had teased at her father's lips. He had found his solution, the way to fulfill his promise to his beloved wife, and that decision was final. Her mother would have been horrified. This was decidedly not what Maria Nordland had meant, and yet to point out that Catarina knew her mother's intentions better than he did would devastate him. So she'd said nothing. Not yet. Not until she got her head around a solution that would untangle the mess that was winding its way around her life.

Since the day her father had announced the marriage proposal, Catarina had buried herself in her books and traveled, trying desperately not to think about this rapidly approaching future. She'd visited her mother's family in Oslo, just to hear them speak the secret language she and her mother had shared. But her cousins' homes were haunted by her mother's ghost, so she'd left them and retreated to the towering place her father had built for her mother, with its mix of Scandinavian sensibilities and an Italian flair for luxury. It was perched on the mountains that rose up from the deep blue Norwegian fjords, dramatic and immovable.

As she listened now to her father wax prosaic over the future that Massimo would bring her, Catarina found herself thinking once again about that place. It was her and her mother's retreat from the world, the place that truly felt like home. It felt like freedom. Catarina alone had inherited it, as her father never had any interest in the stark beauty of his wife's home country. As she nodded at her father's long soliloquies, an answer to her predicament came to her, an answer that would free her from the vise that seemed to be tightening around her chest.

Late that night, long after her father had disappeared down the hallway of the master suite, Catarina packed her bags full of soft wools and fleeces and slipped out of the house. She alerted the pilot of their family's jet that she needed to make a quick trip to Norway, confident that her years of impromptu trips with her mother would mean the crew wouldn't suspect anything out of the ordinary. Definitely not something that her father should be alerted of.

Catarina wasn't running away; at least that was what she told herself on the taxi ride to the airport. She was simply making some space to think. Her father would find her, of course, but with any luck it would take a few days for him to catch up. Knowing her father and his aversion to snow, he was more likely to send someone else to collect his daughter. By then, she would have a plan, because as much as she wanted to please her father, her mother's voice would always speak louder.

"Someday, my little songbird, you must fly on your own." The words still rang in her head. Maybe this wasn't exactly the sort of flight her mother had had in mind, but it was only now that Catarina fully understood why her mother had spoken these words, now that a marriage to Massimo Carandini threatened to take this possibility away.

Catarina had always been a quiet, obedient daughter for her father, but at her core, she was her mother's child. Tomorrow morning, when he found himself alone at the breakfast table, he would be reminded of that fact.

CHAPTER THREE

"I SAID I was not to be disturbed," Massimo said impatiently into the speaker of the phone that sat in the middle of his desk. In front of him lay three newspapers, all featuring speculations of his engagement. While his family's contentious history with the paparazzi had done much damage to both the Carandini name and the brothers' childhoods, Massimo found that some amount of the inevitable publicity could be used strategically. Like, for example, the shot of him pulling up at the d'Avalos family home that he was currently looking at. Massimo was in the middle of reading the article, appropriately flattering thus far, when his assistant's voice had interrupted him.

"Giuseppe d'Avalos is on the line," she said.

Massimo frowned. Was his soon-to-be father-in-law calling to praise the effectiveness of his public relations campaign publicizing their upcoming engagement, or was he calling to manage it? Either way, Massimo wasn't interested in this conversation. He leaned back in his leather chair and ran a hand through his hair. He looked in the direction of the tall windows that opened for a view of Milan's terra-cotta rooftops and green hills in the distance, but he wasn't thinking about the view. Instead, the memory of Catarina's lips on his cheek inexplicably resurrected inside him, followed by the bolt of desire that had pulsed through him, bringing his rational mind to a standstill. Massimo scowled, forcing that thought away.

"Put him through," he grumbled, picking up the receiver of the phone.

"It's Catarina." Giuseppe d'Avalos's usually controlled voice was urgent in Massimo's ear. "She's gone."

Massimo's entire body stilled, and his hand tightened around the phone.

"What do you mean, *gone*?" His voice was as cold as the icy dread that ran through him.

"Catarina did not appear at breakfast, and I found that my pilot had logged an entry for our family's jet last night."

Anger thundered through him. This was not acceptable. Yesterday evening he had spent an hour with his assistant going over the detailed plans of how best to position the release of their engagement. The speculation that had appeared in the morning papers was just the start. There were supper reservations this evening at the iconic Ristorante Emmanuel Rossellini, for example, where their first public appearance would certainly be noted. He had planned to present whatever ring his assistant had purchased to Catarina over dessert. Everything was not only in place, but also set in motion.

Scandal. The word blazed through him. Massimo had spent his entire adult years building up an empire so that he could avoid these kinds of disasters. Now everything he and his brother had worked so hard for could be destroyed in one fell swoop.

"Where did she go?" he asked, keeping his voice under tight control.

"Norway. Her mother had a place in the mountains outside of Tromsø, and she left it to Catarina."

Norway. The flight would be a few hours. Massimo massaged his temple with his free hand. There was still hope of fixing this…situation.

"Have you spoken to her?" he bit out.

"There is a problem with that," said her father cautiously. "Currently, the phones are out of service. The area is prone to strong weather, and this happens more often than not during the storms. I have spoken to the pilot, and I am waiting for the plane to return so someone can gather her up. Discreetly."

The line was silent. Massimo glanced at the Patek Philippe watch ticking away on his wrist. It was just after noon. If he took his own jet, there was still just enough time to bring her back and make their eight o'clock dinner reservations, if he could maneuver through any delays.

Finally, he let out an irritated sigh. "I will go and bring her back myself."

Of course, it would mean canceling all his afternoon meetings. *Like your father used to do*, whispered an insidious voice in the back of his mind.

He flinched, recalling his parents' loud arguments during the intermission of *Tosca* with a flare and drama that had rivaled the action on the main stage. If the theatrics had stayed discreetly between the two of them, maybe his father could have clung on to his family's name. But how many deals had fallen through because his father had canceled a key business meeting to join his wife on a last-minute reconciliation trip after one of the countless times she'd threatened to leave him due to his "neglect"? Of course, he and Alessandro had not missed the fact that neither of his parents had dropped anything when the brothers had gotten kicked out of school.

Massimo gritted his teeth as he tried Catarina's phone number and was immediately directed to voice mail. This engagement was supposed to be a conduit for business, not a hindrance. He would handle Catarina the way he handled everyone else who got in the way of his plans: by making it clear that it was in her best interests to follow the paths he presented to her. Because he knew how to make sure that the people at his command did what he asked them to do. Massimo told himself that this was like any other business crisis he had handled in the past. He would deal with it swiftly and efficiently. And he absolutely would not lose his temper.

Massimo's private jet was ready within the hour, and as the plane flew north, he contemplated his options. Her weakness seemed to be her father, and their marriage agreement was connected to the man's business. He was debating the efficacy of taking a harsher approach with her when his phone rang, and his brother's name appeared on his screen.

"I saw the newspapers this morning," said Alessandro. "Not wasting time with your plans. Efficient as ever."

"There's been a complication," he muttered. "My lovely bride-to-be appears to have fled to Norway."

His brother's laugh traveled through the phone, further grating on his nerves. "You always were a charmer."

The jab irritated Massimo more than usual because of the reality it exposed. He had walked into the library of the d'Avalos estate fully intending to be charming, or at least his best version of it. Somehow, his plans had fallen apart the moment her voice sang through him. And when her lips had brushed against his cheek…

"It's nothing I can't handle," he barked. "We'll return in time for supper at Ristorante Emmanuel Rossellini, as planned."

"I have no doubt," said Alessandro, and Massimo could hear the smile in his brother's voice, crawling farther under his skin. "But I can hear your scowl through the phone line. Maybe you want to work on that before you talk to the woman again."

"I don't need relationship advice from my younger brother," he growled because he was, in fact, a minute older than Alessandro.

This comment only made his brother laugh even louder.

"By all means, use your own…expertise," he said, and Massimo didn't miss the sarcasm that his brother infused in that last word. "As long as this marriage boosts our family's reputation, I don't care how you make it work."

"It will work," he said with finality. "Just take care of anything that is burning this afternoon."

When he ended the call, Massimo reminded himself that he loved his brother. He did, truly, in the same way he loved his grandmother. The two were the only relatives he associated with happy memories from his childhood. When his parents were too busy with their latest dramatic fallout or reunion to be bothered with two young boys, Massimo and Alessandro would spend weeks at their grandparents' sprawling estate on Lake Como, climbing trees, staying out of their thunderous grandfather's path and clinging to their grandmother, elegant, stern and loving. In those earliest memories, neither he nor Alessandro had thought their parents' absences were strange, nor did they think twice about the tempestuous fights that echoed through the house when their parents occasionally graced them with their presence, not when their grandmother would appear with fresh vanilla cake and cold lemonade.

She had protected them, Massimo later realized. His distant grandfather had, too, in his own way, when he'd left the business to the two boys when they came of age, to govern alongside their impulsive and distracted father. The subsequent twelve years since leadership had come into their hands had been spent reviving the business while putting out their parents' fires. Massimo would not allow Catarina to become yet another fire he needed to put out. That was the first message he would make clear when he found her.

As the plane landed on the tiny runway of the Tromsø airport, heavy flakes of snow were falling everywhere, melting on the windows and settling on the snowbanks left by a season's worth of plowing. By the time he walked down the steps and onto the tarmac, the snowfall had shifted from flurries to a storm.

One of his assistants handed him gloves and a change of boots. He waved them off. "I won't need those," he said, picturing the well-groomed path from his car to his favorite resort in the Alps. This would be simple. Quick.

"The storm warning has been upgraded, sir," said the assistant.

Massimo frowned.

"I won't be needing your services until I return," he added, dismissing his staff. "Stand by for my call."

Bringing Catarina back to Milan was a delicate matter, best done alone, no matter how much he trusted his staff. He might even need to adjust his strategy slightly, though first, he needed to figure out why she ran away when the deal was all but signed. He flashed to the smile she had given him just before she had ushered him out of their family's estate, and an unfamiliar wave of uneasiness washed through him. She was not quite the biddable, naive young woman he had taken her for, but this just meant that his new strategy likely needed to involve a more nuanced effort, including some of that…charm his brother mentioned. There was no reason for the wariness this idea seemed to invoke. His intense reaction to her was likely just surprise at his unexpected attraction, nothing more.

A thick layer of snow had settled on the ground as Massimo drove through the narrow streets of Tromsø, passing buildings painted in bright reds and yellows, topped with mounds of white. He crossed a bridge, following the GPS coordinates Giuseppe d'Avalos had given him, and began climbing up the side of the mountain. As he ascended, the lights from the town disappeared, and the only evidence of civilization were the car tracks that guided the way through the newly fallen snow. Great walls of it lined the uphill side of the road, and the downhill side disappeared into a white abyss. The higher his car climbed, the less visible the curves of the mountainside were, as thick, wet flakes hit his windshield. He had rarely driven in more than a centimeter of snow, but he was Massimo Carandini. He could do anything he set his mind to.

When he heard an ominous rumble from the mountainside, he followed his instincts and put his foot on the gas. The SUV fishtailed around the curve, skidding dangerously close to the edge, but he focused on the road in front of him. The GPS told him he was close to the spot where Catarina's mountain home sat, perched on a remote cliffside, so he ignored another rumble from the mountain and sped up. Out of the corner of his eye, he caught a glimpse of movement in the haze of white, uphill from him. It looked as though an enormous snowbank was racing toward him. He slammed his foot on the gas as snow pelted his roof, bumping over mounds as more came crashing down all around him. An avalanche. There was nothing he could do but keep driving, so he raced onward. Too late, he realized he was driving much too fast for the growing layer of wet snow on the road. But he would make it. He was sure of it. The snow was everywhere, covering the windshield now, blocking all hope of seeing what was in front of him. Massimo slammed on the brakes, and the car skidded and spun until it hit something solid. Then everything slammed to a stop.

As the storm picked up, blowing its wind in swirls, what Catarina felt was relief. Phone service was already down, and with any luck, the roads would close soon, too. Planes would be delayed from the heavy spring snow piling on the runway, falling too quickly for the plows to clear.

Catarina sat on a bar stool at the island counter of her kitchen, dressed in her favorite cashmere sweater and leggings, birthday presents from her mother years ago. She warmed her hands with a mug of tea as she looked out the tall windows. In one direction was the barely visible road, and in the other, there was only a hazy white, where on a clear day the fjord would stretch out below her. Today wasn't anywhere near clear.

Thank goodness she had a stocked refrigerator to wait out the storm. On the plane ride from Milan, she had called Signe, their longtime cook, who had filled the refrigerator and cabinets with her favorite Norwegian delicacies as well as ingredients for the meals she would fix after Catarina had settled in. Somehow, Signe had managed to bake cinnamon rolls between the time Catarina had called and the time she had arrived, and she really hoped that Signe hadn't done that in the middle of the night. If she had, at least their family paid her a generous full-time salary for what was very part-time work, so Catarina hoped this made up for the last-minute, late-night inconvenience.

She shivered and shifted her gaze to her third attempt at a fire that was currently smouldering in the fireplace that rose from the opposite side of the great room. This one seemed to be headed in the same direction as the other two. She couldn't get the logs to catch fire properly. It took a while for the central heating to find its way through the many rooms of this house, so for now, she was a bit cold. But at least she was free.

Catarina avoided letting her gaze pause on the piano. There had been a time when music had been her constant companion, playing through her mind. When her mother had entered the last stages of life, that music had faded. Catarina didn't notice until a few weeks after her mother's death, when she sat on the familiar bench, but the music no longer played. She had reached for the keys, playing a few measures by rote, but grief overcame her. After weeks of this, she gave up, and it had been years since she had bothered even to try.

But she wasn't here to think about that time in her life. Instead, Catarina focused on the fact that she'd arrived in the darkness and fallen into bed, burying herself in the billowy layers of down for the most peaceful sleep she'd had in a long time. This morning she had awoken to a breakfast of boiled eggs with caviar, pickled herring on crisp bread and an assortment of fruit, the Norwegian breakfast she and her mother had always eaten when they were here. Now she was working her way through her first cinnamon roll of the day. On her last visit, the ache of loneliness and loss had both pulled her here and then driven her away. Even four years after the funeral, it had felt as if her mother's death took up too much space for anything else to exist in her life.

But this time was different. This time, the ache was tempered by the relief of getting away from her father's autocratic decisions, away from an even more autocratic fiancé. It was a reprieve, a chance to come up with a plan that fulfilled her mother's last requests, both for her father and for herself. Because while her father seemed to believe that a strategic marriage was the path to her happiness, Catarina was sure her mother would agree that there was no happiness in the arrangement Massimo had so clearly laid out for her. As the snow continued to pile up on the windowsills, covering the bushes and trees outside and surrounding her in a soft blanket, thick enough to keep the world at bay, she would come up with a new plan, a plan with her freedom at the center.

She was not ready to think about the dreams that had filled her sleep, dreams of the way Massimo Carandini's gaze had burned into her. But touching him had fully entranced her, the electricity that had skittered over her skin as her lips met his cheek. Her dreams erased the moment everything had shifted to coldness. Instead, in the fantasies born in the deep recesses of her mind, Massimo had angled his head and brought those full, sensual lips to the sensitive skin of her neck, then lower…

Catarina gave herself a little shake. There was no reason to think about this fantasy world her mind had created. Instead, she stared out the window, *not* thinking about Massimo's lips nor his broad shoulders nor any other part of him, parts that she had already imagined in exquisite detail.

These not-thoughts were interrupted by a low rumble from outside, and the floor began to shake underneath her. She grabbed the countertop as she saw the great blanket of snow on the mountain crumbling, dissolving, moving. An avalanche, inevitable in these parts when new snow piled on the thawing layers. Close, but not a threat. More relief flooded inside her. Maybe this one would cover the road for days, giving her more time to come up with a plan.

There was a flash of black that burst through the white haze of the road. An SUV, covered with snow, careened much too fast around the curve of the road. Who was driving in this weather? The car skidded and spun until it hit the snowbank at the base of her driveway with a crunch of metal that reverberated through the triple-paned glass of her kitchen window. The sound was a punch in the gut. Someone was in that car. And she was the only person around for miles.

Catarina abandoned her tea and cinnamon roll and raced to the entrance of the house, the one that had been shoveled and groomed when she'd first arrived but was now covered with snow. She grabbed her pillowy down parka and pulled on the furry boots that covered her calves, then opened the door into the storm. The wind blew the thick flakes in swirls around her as she made her way down the steps, slick with new snow from the storm. She ran down the driveway until she came to the vehicle that was now wedged between the snowbanks, blocking her path out.

She detected no movement inside the car except a haze of white dust that drifted inside, probably from the airbag. Catarina knocked on the window. Nothing. She knocked again, her heart pounding. Still nothing. Then the door creaked until it was wide enough for a person to move through.

When she looked up, her breath caught in her throat. Massimo Carandini appeared out of the dust. He climbed out from behind the airbag, stepping into the snow, raising himself to his full height. He was standing so close to her, the snow dancing around him, landing in his tousled hair and on the shoulders of his woollen coat.

Then she saw the blood. His hair had hidden it, but a stream of red was coming from his forehead near his hairline. Catarina meant to speak, but her voice died in her throat as the intensity of his stare hit her. His eyes were dark, and she felt that fire from those first moments after they met buzzing between them. He gazed at her with something she might have called *wonder* if she didn't know better. Still, a rush of desire ran through her, unwanted and ill timed.

Massimo continued to gaze at her with a strange, searching expression, like he wasn't quite sure what to do with her. He stared at her with a focus in his dark brown eyes that made her feel as if he truly saw her. It took her breath away, so she found herself looking everywhere but his eyes, at his silky black hair that was collecting wet flakes of snow, at his charcoal-gray jacket, appropriate for a cool night on Lake Como rather than a blizzard in the remote mountains of Norway.

And then there were his hands, those lovely, long fingers, completely bare. Who drove into a Nordic blizzard without a hat or gloves?

Massimo Carandini did. Only an arrogant man with the confidence of a king would assume that he was above Mother Nature. Also, he had just crashed his car, she reminded herself.

"What are you doing here?" she whispered, and her cheeks burned in the cold air.

The sound of her voice seemed to startle him, and whatever openness she had seen closed. The intensity of his eyes turned to something more ominous.

"You forced me to follow you to the Arctic and now the car is..." He gestured at the airbag.

She blinked. "I *forced* you to come?"

This was rich. He blamed her for following her and seemed to be on the verge of blaming her for the state of his car. This was the man who had just recklessly driven to her cabin in the middle of a snowstorm, and yet he made it sound like she was somehow putting him out.

He checked his watch, then glared at her impatiently. "We still have enough time to make our supper reservation at Ristorante Emmanuel Rossellini if we leave now."

"In Milan?" Catarina was aware that her usually tempered voice betrayed hints of incredulity. "And how do you suggest we make our way through the avalanche that you just barely escaped?"

"A helicopter could land somewhere in this open space, for example," he said, gesturing into the white swirl of the snowstorm.

"And how do you suggest we call one?"

His answer was a glare that suggested further irritation. He pointed to her house that towered in the nothingness of the white snow that was coming down increasingly harder. "You must have some way of getting out of here."

Catarina took a deep breath, trying to control her exasperation. "I'm afraid I don't, as we are currently in the middle of a blizzard. I am going to interpret this magical thinking of yours as a possible consequence of the head injury you have sustained."

He glared at her. "I have no idea what you are talking about."

"You're bleeding." She hadn't meant to soften her voice, but every time she caught a glimpse of the red on his forehead, something tugged at her gut. *He's just a man.*

"I'm not bleeding," he snapped.

She ignored his comment and reached up to touch the trickle of blood. This was a mistake. When she touched his skin, the electric pull between them sparked back to life. His eyes narrowed, as if he had felt it, too, and was blaming it on her yet again. She swallowed, shoving away the uncomfortable heat inside, and turned her hand to show him the blood. He didn't speak. They stood in some sort of silent battle until she could no longer ignore his bare hands, exposed to the wind and cold.

"You need to get out of this weather," she finally said, then indicated up the hill, in the direction of her cabin. "You might as well come in. Do you have anything in the car that you need? Perhaps clothes or toiletries?" she asked.

"I brought nothing. We are not staying."

"Indeed," she said. Had he actually suffered from a concussion, or was he just so arrogant as to assume that even a snowstorm was not an insurmountable hurdle for following through with the plan he had engineered? Though Massimo was undoubtedly well-traveled, clearly, he had never been to a remote fjord, far from cities and servants at his beck and call. This remoteness was what her mother had loved best about the place and, quite possibly, what had made her father stay away. Here, the forces of nature did not bend to money and power, and her father preferred to stay in the realm where it did. Massimo was likely the same, and he would understand his predicament soon enough. She knew better than to press the issue.

"Someone should call about my car," he said, nodding in the direction of the mess of crunched metal and shattered glass that was the front of the SUV.

Someone meaning…her? Catarina resisted an eye roll because twenty-four years of managing her father had taught her to keep her tone unfailingly polite. Even when the situation did not call for it. "Unfortunately, as I mentioned, the mobile towers are down at the moment."

She waited for his reply, but it didn't come. He simply gazed out into the blizzard.

"Shall we go inside?" she asked, giving him another one of her patient smiles.

He ignored her suggestion and gestured again at the

endless white landscape in that imperious way of his, as if the entire world was at his bidding. As if, even here, in the middle of a blizzard on an empty mountainside, all it took was a mere flick of his finger to set into motion whatever he willed. As if he expected her to respond to him the same way.

"The road," he said. "Where does it lead?"

It was the oddest question to ask. He didn't choose the obvious one, which was, why did you leave so suddenly in the middle of the night, on the eve of our official engagement? Actually, she was expecting something more demanding, something that started with *how dare you...?*

Catarina sighed. This interaction only validated her decision to flee. How could she marry this arrogant, imperious man? Still, she drew on her years of patience and ingrained manners and answered him. "There's not much that way, just a smattering of houses close to the border of Sweden."

Massimo frowned, but said nothing more.

"Let's go inside," she said gently, coaxing. "It's quite chilly out here."

He looked a bit startled by her last comment, and she could feel the intensity of his gaze return fully to her. Then Massimo unfastened the top button of his coat. He moved on to the second one.

"What are you doing?" she asked quickly.

He looked at her with a kind of exaggerated patience, as if his actions were perfectly obvious. "You are cold, so I am giving you my coat."

His gaze was almost a glare, as if it hadn't crossed

his mind that her concern about the cold wasn't for herself. She wasn't sure what to do with that, so at odds with the rest of their conversation.

"Keep your coat on," she said urgently. "Please."

She pressed her bare hand against his long fingers. Her breath caught in her throat as the electric desire buzzed across her skin. She pulled her hand away, refusing to meet his gaze. It was dangerous to touch this man. Despite the cold, the rush of heat shot through her. She would avoid it at all costs, she promised herself, even if she was snowbound in her cabin with him.

Catarina turned away and said over her shoulder, "Follow me."

CHAPTER FOUR

Massimo had expected tears. He had expected demands for tokens of affection, perhaps the ring she had mentioned at their meeting the day before to solidify their engagement. But Catarina didn't throw strategically selected pieces of her family's heirloom porcelain, nor did she collapse into a breathless display of distress on her favorite chaise longue, the way Massimo had seen his mother do the moment his father walked in the door. He had at the very least expected to find Catarina looking distraught. However, for a moment she had looked almost…irritated at his appearance in her driveway. That couldn't be right.

But that inexplicable expression had so quickly disappeared, replaced by the veneer of politeness she so expertly wielded. Was she just disappointed that the unfortunate crash of his car hadn't allowed for her best, most dramatic performance? That seemed the most likely explanation. Catarina had claimed that she didn't crave the spotlight, but plenty of his mother's performances had taken place out of the public eye. Catarina could simply be reconsidering her approach.

Massimo found that his temper was rising at yet another unexpected complication. She seemed to excel at creating these complications, he thought bitterly, particularly for someone selected for the lack of complications she posed. He followed Catarina along the driveway as he scanned the area for possible ways to leave. Though this entire situation that she had forced him into was frustratingly inconvenient, he would not let Catarina destroy the plans he had so carefully orchestrated.

Snow had seeped into his leather shoes, leaving them cold and wet, and each slippery step in the new snow sparked the temper that still threatened to flare inside him. His temple throbbed, and he brought his hand to the spot where Catarina had touched his forehead just moments ago. He could still feel the echo of her fingers against his skin, the soft brush that shimmered inside him. He took away his hand and frowned at the traces of blood on his fingers. Another wave of uneasiness washed over him. Had he misread her middle-of-the-night disappearance? Did she flee not to get his attention but to escape the marriage? That would be… inconvenient. The thought triggered the unsettled feeling in his gut that had persisted since his phone call with d'Avalos. He needed to get them back on track, which meant figuring out what she was after.

As they walked up the driveway, the house took shape, rising up in the blowing snow. Though no one would call a place of this size and grandeur a chalet, the building had echoes of its humbler version of the mountain cabins he had passed along the road. But this was a home, stately, clad in varnished wood with long windows and a towering peaked roof of metal, clearly made to withstand storms much worse than this. The design was clean and deceptively simple. Catarina led him along a snow-covered path and up the steps to a covered porch at the entry of the house. She opened the thick wooden door, and he followed her inside.

The front hallway opened into an enormous room lined with windows, with a stone fireplace at its center. The diffuse light from the snow outside came in through the tall windows, giving the place an almost mystical glow. He frowned and scanned the entryway, focusing on the only part that stood out, an abandoned pile of luggage, handbags, scarves and other miscellaneous items in the corner. His gaze moved to Catarina as she took off her outer layers and hung them in some sort of metal box in the corner of the hallway, leaving her dressed in a cloud of a sweater that hugged her breasts and accentuated her narrow waist. His body reacted. Her lush curves were on full display, and suddenly Massimo was all too aware that they were stuck together in a remote place.

"You can hang your coat in this drying closet," she said as she turned the knob, and the appliance came to life. Then she frowned at his shoes. "Though I don't think it can do anything about those."

Massimo hung up his coat, shoes and soaked socks in the closet, then followed her through to a large room that spanned the entire length of the house. A dining room table was positioned at one end, and across the broad space was the fireplace, with a grand piano in the far corner. The exposed beams across the towering ceiling were offset by the white walls and wide-planked wooden floors, covered with rugs patterned in reds, blues and whites. She gestured to the floor-to-ceiling windows.

"When the snow lets up, the sofa provides a view across the fjord and up the mountains on the other side," she said, as if he was a weekend guest stopping by for a tour.

She pointed him toward the kitchen, then disappeared in a different direction. The tile was cool under his feet as he took in the sleek white cabinets, accents of light wood and sparkling steel appliances that surrounded him. On the counter, there were glass containers of baked goods, cookies and buns of some sort, and a few dirty dishes were abandoned by the sink. No shards of family porcelain were in sight, nor was there evidence of domestic help. Massimo didn't know what to make of this scene, but he braced himself for the inevitable onslaught of her emotional upheaval, whenever it came.

Catarina returned to the kitchen, her cheeks flushed from the cold, her hair tousled, and the scent he remembered was everywhere, roses and something from the sea. A bolt of lust flashed too quickly to resist, and the warning that chimed through him was just as strong. But Massimo was not his father, who so eagerly responded to his mother's every whim. He would make that perfectly clear.

She was holding a flat metal first aid box, a pair of thick, navy-blue socks and a hideous Christmas-themed jumper. She placed all three items on the island counter and smiled at him with a glint of challenge in her eyes.

"I'm afraid the place hasn't fully warmed up yet, so I brought you an extra layer from my father's closet," she said. "And in case you're concerned, none of it has been worn."

He gave the jumper a disdainful glance. "I can't imagine why."

She rested both hands on the island counter and leveled him with her gaze.

"Why did you come?" she asked. Her voice held a hint of temper.

This reaction he recognized. This he could handle. Massimo took a step forward, and he bit back a smile when her breath caught and her cheeks darkened with heat. His own body stirred in response, but he didn't allow his attention to stray to her lush lips that begged to be kissed, nor did he let himself tangle his fingers in her silky hair. Not yet, at least. Because he had her exactly where he wanted her. "Should I not follow my runaway fiancée?"

She swallowed and raised an eyebrow. "Are we engaged? I guess I must have missed the moment I said yes, among all the fanfare of your proposal."

Her tone had returned to unfailing politeness, the way it had the night before, and there was no mistaking the cutting sarcasm laced in these words. The comment triggered a bizarre urge to snap back at her, to make clear that their arrangement was supposed to be settled. It was also supposed to be convenient, a descriptor that she was doing her best to defy.

"Did your father keep you in the dark about the nature of my proposal?" he said, keeping his voice silky smooth. She looked away when he mentioned her father, so he continued. "Did he promise you something that I did not deliver?"

"Of course not. You were exactly what I should have expected." She managed to make this sound like an insult.

"And yet, something did not meet your satisfaction," he continued. "Maybe you were still hoping for a fairy-tale marriage?"

Her cheeks flushed, and he could see he was on the right track.

"You have nothing to worry about," she said, and the corners of her mouth turned down. "I have no illusions of a happy ending between us."

"There will be plenty of happy endings between us, *cara*," he said, letting his voice turn rough with the fire that blazed through him at these words. "That is a promise. But I am a far cry from Prince Charming. As you might have noted."

Her eyes flashed with unmistakable heat, and he felt a surge of satisfaction. He had found his way under her polite facade. But Massimo's body surged with anticipation, and he flashed back to the moment her lips brushed against his cheek back in her library. Her touch had been dangerously electric. He held back the urge to frown and focused on the plan he could not lose sight of.

"As soon as this—" he glanced out the window, into the haze of snow "—is over and we have phone service, I will call a helicopter, and we will fly home then head directly to the restaurant, where I will propose appropriately, with all the fanfare you require. And, if you choose, we can begin right away with the happy endings you claim you are not interested in."

Catarina appeared wholly unmoved by his plan. She lifted her chin, exposing more of the slim column of her neck.

"While we are setting expectations," she said in that prim voice of hers, "I should warn you that restoring phone service will likely take days, as will clearing the road from the avalanche."

He tried to tamp down his frustrations. "I am leaving for Tokyo tomorrow, and that absolutely cannot be postponed."

"I apologize for the inconvenience," she said, and a hint of exasperation laced her polite tone, "though I cannot help but point out that coming here was entirely your choice. In fact, you might note that I left in a manner that suggests I did not want to be followed."

The idea rattled through him, triggering another wave of uneasiness. Her words stirred up a strange mix of emotions that felt a little too close to disappointment for his liking.

"Though I am always pleased to see you, of course," she added sweetly.

"Of course," he bit out.

Had she truly not wanted him to come? It should have been a relief that she hadn't shown any signs of the showy hysterics and demands that his mother made. He told himself it was proof that he had, in fact, made the right choice in marriage partners. This was a woman who avoided the spotlight, something she herself had emphasised. She wouldn't turn dinner parties and galas into a forum to demand his public fealty to her. This, above all, was most important. Still, he couldn't help but note the way she was provoking him, which led him to another possibility. Maybe she was playing the same games as his mother, though with more cunning and restraint. If so, she had succeeded in getting his attention, he thought with a frown.

"Why did you run?" he asked, his voice low and deceptively calm.

"I didn't run. I retreated to gather my thoughts." Her eyelashes fluttered as she stared up at him, defiance shining in her eyes.

"We had an arrangement, which you backed out of." His voice was low and ominous. "I would hate to think that this is how you approach your commitments. Your father was certainly displeased."

The polite smile fell from her lips, and for a moment, in its place was something that looked like pain. Massimo felt an unwanted twist in the gut. He told himself he didn't regret his comment. He was entering negotiations, just the way he had intended. And yet, her expression made him feel distinctly…uncomfortable.

Catarina took a deep breath and added, "I needed time to consider my options. I still have options at this point, don't I?"

"Everyone has options, *cara*," he said, keeping his voice smooth. "Some lead down easier roads than others."

She licked her lips. It was an unconscious action, and yet his body responded to it. "Maybe I found that I am less interested in easier roads, no matter how smooth they are. We all choose roads that lead us to the desired destinations, do we not?"

"That assumes you have a map. But no one can be certain of where a road will take them," he said wryly, "no matter how carefully they choose it."

The events of the past day had reminded him of this lesson.

"Thank you so much for this piece of wisdom, which I will, of course, consider thoroughly. However, I'm afraid neither of us has many options at the moment," she said crisply. "In the meantime, let me bandage your forehead."

She reached up toward his face, but when her fingers came close to touch him, the hum of attraction that he had been ignoring surged. Catarina pulled her hand away, as if she had felt it, too, and for a moment, uncertainty flashed in her eyes. She swallowed, and he had the distinct impression she was silently talking herself into something. Then she added, "Signe would never make my favorite cinnamon rolls again if she had to clean trails of blood through the house."

She waved her hand around, as if the entire ground floor of this enormous place was at risk. Then she got to work.

Massimo studied her as she opened the first aid box on the granite countertop and sized him up, like she was taking in his height. Catarina frowned, then dragged a chair over from the table. He sat, which put him in the unfortunate position of being eye level with her breasts. They were pert and full beneath the soft cloud of a jumper she was wearing, and he found himself imagining the way they would feel in his hands. In his mouth. A stir in his groin cut through the cool sting of the alcohol wipe on his forehead. This was certainly not how he had seen this day playing out. And yet, he had to admit his situation had sparked a note of curiosity in him. Also, he didn't mind the view.

"You still haven't told me what you want," he said, softening his tone, noting the way her pulse at the tender base of her neck skittered each time he spoke.

Catarina swept a hand around the expansive room, filled with the kind of understated luxury that left no doubt about her singularly privileged upbringing. "This is all mine. I want for nothing."

There was a wryness in her voice, an irony that suggested there were, in fact, things she wanted. And Massimo found himself wondering what those things were and how he could tease this information out of her. He flashed her an indulgent smile. "Indeed. You have planes and houses at your disposal, though there appears to be an oversight in the domestic worker department."

His gaze flickered to the dirty dishes, then in the direction of the front entryway, where she had left her belongings in a heap. When his gaze returned to her, he caught a hint of amusement in the curve of her lush lips.

"Maybe I prefer to be alone," she said tartly as she patted his forehead with the alcohol wipe.

"Maybe. But you could have simply attended our engagement dinner first," he said, his voice deceptively calm. "Surely you didn't disappoint your father just for one extra day of 'me time.'"

The amusement disappeared from her expression, and despite the fact that he was trying to get under her skin, he found he didn't like this change. Once again, it was the mention of her father that triggered another flash of discomfort. This time, she didn't try to hide it.

"You know nothing about me," she said, her jaw tight as she reached for a bandage.

"How fortunate that we have the rest of our lives to learn as much—or as little—about each other as we choose," he said, a smug smile tugging at his lips. "I am certain that we can come to an understanding that allows for plenty of alone time, if that is what you desire. You'll find that I will not require your presence too often."

"What a relief," she said, not bothering to disguise her sarcasm. She let out a huff of a breath. "I've patched you up, but I probably should check for a concussion."

"I do *not* have a concussion." He and his brother had gotten into more than enough fights in the back halls of their boarding school to gauge that this was far from a concussion. "But feel free to continue your...inspection of me." He found that he was enjoying all her focused attention.

She took a step back, and her gaze traced his face until he could almost swear it settled on his lips. The stir of desire surged inside him, and he allowed himself to lean into that feeling. Massimo had not forgotten that moment in the d'Avalos library, when she'd looked at him like she was overflowing with innocent desire.

Her long, slim throat was exposed, and the pulse at the base of it was even faster than before. The vulnerability with her father was difficult to wield and certainly contained many unknowns. This baser kind of vulnerability he understood completely. He knew from a lifetime of watching his parents that passion could override everything else. He'd watched his father make decisions that put that reckless desire before his sons, his future and his family name. Maybe desire could make Catarina reckless, too.

Her eyes begged for things she probably didn't even know how to name. There was naked, raw want in her gaze, want that was already overriding her desire to keep her distance. Massimo told himself he knew exactly how to handle this, to keep it under control and use it as a tool. Even if the situation had veered much too far from his control today. But he could sort that out later.

Instead, he focused on the tempting heat that sparked in her gaze. He leaned forward and let his eyes dip to her mouth, watching the way it parted slowly as he lowered his head. Her eyes widened as he closed the distance between them, but she didn't move away. Instead, she leaned closer, bringing those lush lips only inches away from his. Her soft breaths came faster, brushing over his skin, kicking his own desire up a notch. But this was nothing he couldn't handle.

"What are you doing?" she whispered.

Though she was innocent, Massimo had no doubt she knew what he was doing. He let a satisfied grin spread across his lips.

"You treated my wound," he said, his voice rasping deeper. "I'm thanking you properly."

And then he closed the last distance and let his mouth press against hers. He had meant it to just be a brush of his lips, a temptation of sorts to hint at the untapped pleasure between them that could lure her into submission. But the moment his lips touched hers, they were suddenly back in her library, with Catarina's voice ringing inside him, so lovely and captivating, and the smell of aging leather contrasting with roses and the salty sea-like scent that flooded him when she was close. His last coherent thought was that she had somehow managed to turn the tables on him, that he was losing control. Then everything came together in a resounding chorus that rang inside him once again, the song he had been resisting since she had appeared surrounded in a halo of snow: *mine*.

His mouth brushed over hers just once, but the caress of his lips triggered an earthquake of unsettling heat that raced through her body. Before she could steady herself enough to fully register these sensations, the heat turned to an ache that pooled in her breasts and between her legs. *Just a man*, she tried to remind herself. And yet, as this imposing man hovered over her, these sensations threated to overwhelm her body. There was no *just* about him.

Since Massimo had stepped out of the car, she had watched a combination of frustration and confusion flicker across his face, but she had also seen hints of what she could have sworn was curiosity. Interest. Maybe she had misjudged him…or maybe this was her imagination, triggered by the idea of fairy-tale marriages. And happy endings, she reminded herself. That had set off a molten cascade through her that gathered deep in her belly. Now, standing so close, she wasn't prepared for the way his eyes narrowed imperceptibly with desire, the way they turned dark, filling with a bottomless hunger that called to her. She wasn't prepared for the craving it awoke in her, the way it cut through marriage bargains and stifling expectations, calling to a part of her that couldn't resist feeding that hunger.

She pulled back slightly, taking him in. Up close, Massimo was breathtakingly beautiful. Until now, Catarina had not fully registered the way this man made it feel as though the ground under her feet was unstable. The cut she had attended to wasn't his first injury, she noted. Above his left eyebrow, a thin white line marred the bronze skin of his forehead, jagged and long-since healed, and his nose had a rugged look to it, as if it had been broken at some point. The remains of old injuries only served to highlight the beauty of his face, the sharp angles of his cheekbones, the square line of his jaw, the impossibly long lashes that softened the brooding intensity of his eyes. And then there were his lips. They were two sensual, carnal promises that lit her body and left her fingers trembling with an ache to touch them. God, she wanted to touch them. She was caught between temptation and warning, because though she did not know exactly what those lips promised, she knew she wanted it. Maybe even needed it.

Catarina had been on dates, of course, with appropriate men, and on the whole, she found these dinners exactly what they were supposed to be: entertaining and civilized. Somehow, she had mistaken these experiences for attraction. But what she'd felt during those well-mannered evenings had nothing in common with this sensation that her body was not enough to contain the heat that rushed through her. When he was sitting on the chair, looking at her as she tended to his wound, Massimo's nearness had felt uncomfortably intimate. But now, as he towered over her, she felt a different kind of intimacy, a different promise that made her shiver. It was a promise too much to even contemplate and she instinctually knew she needed to stay far away.

Catarina was so aware of how close they were and how alone they were, so far from the structures of her life. This house in the mountains was a place that was her own, a place that had always meant independence, but right now, she was so far from the freedom she craved. And though she tried to tell herself that she would run again from him if she could, she knew that this was a lie.

Back in her library, she had still been in the thrall of her fantasies, partly rooted in the fairy tale of a man she had seen from afar at sixteen, and partly rooted in the freedom that she assumed would come from that marriage. But here in the mountains, without her father nearby, watching to assess the probable outcomes of a favorable marriage contract, Massimo Carandini was viscerally real.

She wanted to move closer. Her whole body was alive with a craving that narrowed her focus to this man in front of her. What would happen if she kissed the hollow at the base of his neck, the place where his heartbeat ticked its relentless reminder that he was a red-blooded man whose physical presence called to her?

He was hovering right above her, his lips just out of reach, and a sudden panic welled up inside her. Would he pull back? Would *she* pull away if she thought any of this through? Before doubts could take over, she slid her hand down his cheek, feeling the smooth, soft skin, where it met the roughness of the stubble. The heat of him shot through her body, and she felt more alive than she had in years.

This was that craving that had swept through her in her library, a room filled with the oppressive weight of her mother's death and her father's overbearing designs on her life. This was the craving she had felt when she had kissed him, that gentle brush of her lips against his skin. She was alive and not alone, and even if this feeling only lasted for this fleeting moment, she would not back away. Catarina cupped her other hand to his cheek, holding his face in her hands, and urged his lips back to hers. Just one more time, she thought, just so she didn't doubt it was real, the way she did last time. Just so she didn't regret letting this moment slip away. Because whatever regrets she had over the past twenty-four hours, his kiss definitely wasn't one of them.

Her heart pounded in her chest as she rose to her toes. It was hard to breathe when she was this close, and yet it felt impossible to pull away. His eyes narrowed, as if warning her away, then widened when she didn't retreat. She focused on his lips. They seemed to call to her, so she answered, pressing her mouth against his. He didn't move. He didn't respond, and for a moment, she thought he would push her away. But suddenly, before she could sense the shift in him, his arms slipped around her neck and into her hair, and he was kissing her back. Sensations rushed through her body, flashes of heat that lived just under her skin, addictive and demanding. He parted his lips, and she gasped as his tongue swept against hers, so intimate and sexual. A craving was building deep inside her, a longing, a chasm that had opened inside her. She *needed*. Massimo let out a low rumble, somewhere between pleasure and frustration. Then his strong hands moved through her hair and pulled her closer. He tilted his head to deepen the kiss, and all semblance of thoughts disappeared.

Then, suddenly and achingly abruptly, he pulled back. His hands braced her shoulders, as if he was physically forcing himself away, despite the connection that sparked and sizzled between them. There was a wild look in his eyes, something new and so out of control that it made her breath catch in her throat. The sound seemed to break the connection. The wild look disappeared, morphing into something more familiar. It was triumph.

"What are you playing at, *cara*?" he said in a lazy drawl.

She blinked in confusion.

"Playing at?" she finally whispered. Her voice shook, and she was so far from under control.

"You tell me you didn't want me to follow you here, and then you kiss me as if you're inviting me into your bed." His eyes flared with lust as he spoke those words, as if he, unwillingly, was thinking about their kiss again, and exactly where it could lead. He shook his head, and that sheen of desire disappeared from his eyes.

"Which is it, Catarina?" he said, his voice low and seductive. "What do you really want?"

She stared at him. What *was* she doing? As a child, her mother had encouraged her to follow her desires and passions, but what would her mother say if she saw Catarina now, awash with a hunger that had pulled her under for a few blissful moments? All the details about this man, details she had been trying so hard to ignore since he arrived, bombarded her: the way his shoulders stretched against the seams of his well-tailored shirt; the hints of laugh lines at the corners of his eyes; the traces of whiskers on his clean-shaven skin; and the scent of him, with hints of pine, masculine in a way that felt undeniably sexual. Now that she had kissed him, she couldn't stop thinking about this. This was something elemental, as if a part of her was opening, a part that she never knew existed. Also, she was snowbound with Massimo inside this house. There was no way they could leave tonight, which meant they would be spending the night under the same roof. Just the two of them. The night before, when she had fallen into bed alone, this towering house had felt as if it echoed with emptiness. Now Massimo's presence made it feel stiflingly small.

Everything about him felt sexual, and it lit her body on fire in a way that she could not ignore. And yet, she had to. This was the man who wanted to take away her freedom, she reminded herself.

Massimo raised his eyebrows expectantly, as if daring her to answer him. But she was in control of her voice. Her voice was one of the tools she had learned to use, a skill, if properly honed, that had the power to cut through the forces that steered her life. Her mother had taught her this lesson. A voice was power, a power that could be wielded within the confines of Catarina's position. Though she had none of her mother's ambition to sing on stage, she had learned to sing in her own ways.

Catarina felt a sudden urge to laugh, but it came out as a bitter, humorless sound of exasperation. "What am I playing at? I recommend you reassess the situation."

She didn't even know where to start with how wrong his accusation of *playing* was. Yes, she had continued his kiss, but only after he'd kissed her and looked at her in a way that made her feel like he was going to devour her. What was his expectation? That she would sit back and wait for him to take the lead on everything, starting with the terms of their marriage all the way down to how and when they kissed? How very arrogant of him, to assume that even that last space between their lips should have been under his control, that she should act according to his unspoken parameters. It was almost as if he did not consider her as a person, with her own will. This was her worst nightmare. So why did her body burn like he was exactly what she wanted? She pushed that question out of her mind.

Her breaths were still coming fast from the kiss as she looked up into his dark eyes, full of recrimination.

"You kissed me." She had meant it as an accusation, but her voice had taken on a husky tone that made this statement sound more like an invitation. She should hate this man for whatever game he was playing or manipulation he was trying, but her gaze flicked down to his lips again, and a shudder of pleasure ran through her. He saw it, too, and he released her and stepped away, as if she were made of fire and he had just been burnt.

"We will save this discussion for later, when you can be more rational about this," he said darkly.

This last sentence seemed perfectly designed to spark her temper, despite all the years of perfecting the art of holding it in. It was yet more evidence that he had mistaken a quiet, media-shy daughter for an obedient ornament. But just because she didn't love attention didn't mean she lacked a will of her own. It didn't make her an unformed piece of clay to mold into whatever shape he chose.

She had to get away from him before she made any further mistakes—because the kiss had, in fact, been a mistake. But Catarina was better at dodging problems rather than confronting them head-on. It was how she had ended up in this mess in the first place. She had run from her father instead of confronting him about the marriage arrangement. But it was too late for regrets in that department. She needed a better plan. She needed space to cool down and think.

"Why don't I show you to a room," she said, then added, "You can attend to some of your *important* business."

He was watching her in that calculating way he had, as if assessing her motives. Before he could say anything more, she took a deep breath and forced a long-practiced calm she didn't feel into her voice. "We are stuck here for the foreseeable future. The house is big enough for us to stay out of each other's way, and the generator should keep us warm for a while."

His eyes narrowed, and she answered with a placid smile, then turned away and started for the staircase. At the top of the steps, the hallway spread out in two directions. She turned to the right and walked the length of the hall to the end. Next to her, Massimo loomed. She wasn't even facing him, and yet Catarina had never been so aware of another man.

Turning the handle, the door swung open and Catarina walked into the bright room, lit with the fall of the snow. "Everything you need should be here."

A king-size bed in rough-hewn wood was the centerpiece of the large room, and it was surrounded by a dresser, small tables and a rocking chair in the same wood. Over the bed hung a large painting of their fjord, the deep blues of the water and sky contrasting with the peaks of the forest of pine trees and stark gray rock. In the middle of the wooden floor was a soft white carpet.

Catarina had not entered the guest room in years, and as her gaze swept across the room, she caught a glimpse of the single framed photo on the rough-hewn wooden table next to the rocking chair. It was of Catarina and her mother, sitting on a stretch of bare rock at the top of a mountain not far from the house. Catarina's aunt and two cousins had visited from Oslo the summer before her mother's diagnosis, and the five of them had wandered up paths and stopped for a picnic lunch to take in the panoramic views. Her aunt had meant to capture the stark beauty of the landscape, but what the photo captured for Catarina was a sense of *before*, a time that sometimes felt like it no longer belonged to her.

Massimo's gaze was on the photo, too. Then he looked at her with an expression that she couldn't read.

"I trust you to make yourself at home," she said quickly and turned for the door.

"If I need anything, I'll find you," he said, and his voice stirred inside her, sending a hot lick of desire through her body that echoed far too long.

CHAPTER FIVE

SHE REALLY SHOULD check on him, Catarina thought as she laid her book on the side table, the one she had been staring at unproductively for too long. Instead of reading, she had found herself thinking about how silent it had been in Massimo's room. Her mind flitted to her previous worry that the accident had caused a concussion. The right thing to do was to check on him, she told herself. For his own good. Not because of this desire he sparked in her. Not because of the memory of his fingers against her scalp as he wove them through her hair and then the startling heat of his mouth as he took hers. The word *took* was the only way to describe what he did with his hands and his mouth. Catarina had thought she'd known the meaning of that word, but his kiss had destroyed her old understanding and rebuilt it into something new, something that enticed her as much as it made her wary. Because she had wanted him to take more.

But she was checking on him out of concern, she repeated to herself as she headed out of her room and down the long hallway. She knocked on the door, and the sound echoed through the quiet house. He didn't answer. Catarina knocked again, and when he didn't answer immediately, she rested her hand on the door handle. But as she turned the knob, the handle was yanked out of her hand.

Catarina's breath caught in her throat. Massimo was standing so close, and a spark of electric heat shot through her. The stark planes of his face were tight, and his gaze was inscrutable. A bump had formed on his head, and Catarina detected dark shadows under his eyes, as if he hadn't slept well, even though his broad shoulders suggested a kind of power that wouldn't budge for such worldly obstacles as a car crash. Or a snowstorm. Or a wayward almost-fiancée.

"Yes?" He used that same sultry tone he had in the kitchen, and his deep voice sent another spark of awareness through her.

"I was just checking to see if you were—" she hesitated. *Conscious* didn't seem to be the right way to finish this sentence "—warm enough?" Belatedly, Catarina registered that he was wearing the tacky Christmas jumper she had left for him, along with the socks. He lifted a brow, as if daring her to comment further on his attire.

"Right. You look fine," she continued quickly. "Also, our cook stocked the refrigerator with food when you are hungry. And if you need anything else…"

"For example?" His voice was so distracting that, for a moment, she wondered if he was…flirting with her? The idea was a spark inside that she knew she should ignore. And yet, she didn't.

"Perhaps more Christmas attire?" she asked archly.

She could have sworn the corners of his mouth twitched up in amusement. "Very generous offer. I'll keep that in mind."

She felt his penetrative gaze bore into her as she walked away.

All afternoon she found herself distracted by this conversation. He couldn't have been flirting with her, could he? Their first meeting the day before suggested that Massimo Carandini was constitutionally unequipped for such frivolities, and yet that spark inside her wouldn't go away.

Not even later that night, when she closed her book again. The house was quiet. In fact, she hadn't heard a sound from Massimo's side of the hall in a long time. She flashed back to his tall frame in the doorway of his room, the hint of amusement teasing his mouth… and the bandage on his forehead. This man had been in a car accident, she reminded herself, which probably meant she should have checked on him more carefully earlier instead of getting so distracted by, well, everything. He had, of course, appeared to be the pinnacle of health. Still, now that she thought about it, she definitely should see if he was all right, especially considering the warnings she was remembering about head injuries and sleep.

Catarina rose from the soft comfort of her reading chair and crept into the hallway until she reached the door to Massimo's room. She stopped and gave the door a gentle tap. Just to make sure he was fine, she told herself. The house was still and silent. She tried again, this time more forcefully. Nothing. If he was asleep, then she really should wake him, just to make sure. Catarina knocked one more time and was answered with silence, so she took a deep breath and entered the bedroom.

The snow lit the walls in a silvery glow, and the light from the windows cast shadows that emphasized the cut of his cheekbones, the angle of his jaw. At rest, he looked so much more peaceful. The intensity of his gaze was gone, as was the frown he gave her so often. The glimmer of the snow brightened the white duvet and shimmered on Massimo's bare skin. So much of his bare skin was exposed. Her heart took off in her chest, sending a wave of tingling desire that settled in her core, racing toward what Catarina had spent too much time pushing away. *Don't get distracted this time*, she chided herself as she crossed the room. *Just wake him, then exit.*

Up close, the silvery light highlighted the curves and shadows of his muscular stomach and chest. He lay on his back, shirtless, with one arm tossed over his head, revealing a patch of silky hair under his arm that somehow made him look both aggressively masculine and also vulnerable. He had another patch of dark hair across his chest and a third trail that invited her gaze down to where the covers began, as if begging her to contemplate what lay beneath. A shiver of desire ran through her, hot and electric. *Just a man. A man who could have a head injury*, she reminded herself sternly.

Her mind was suddenly flooded with things she wanted to do, perhaps trace the hair on the torso to test its texture or maybe bring her lips to his skin just to see how he tasted. But one did not do these things to a sleeping man, even if said man was slated to become one's fiancé. *Wake him and exit*, she repeated to herself.

But she was wary of touching him. Every inch of his body felt aggressively sexual. With an unsteady breath, she settled on the bed next to him, her hip so close to his chest. Heat from his body radiated through the silk of her pajamas, reminding her once again that this was not a dream. She watched the gentle rise and fall of his chest as he breathed, and she studied the harsh planes of his cheeks and nose and forehead, softened in his sleep. She studied the defined muscles of his shoulders, taking in their hard solidity as more electric heat zapped through her. Her breaths came faster as the need grew inside her. She had the urge to press her body against his to soothe this ache in her belly, between her legs.

Which was completely inappropriate. Massimo was *sleeping*, for goodness' sake. Catarina raised her hand to her chest, as if to steady the flutter of her own heart, but when she moved, she could have sworn that his muscles tensed. She froze.

"Massimo?" she whispered.

Nothing. She was imagining things again. Just her own guilty conscience, she decided.

She swallowed, steeling herself for her reaction to the feel of his smooth skin under her fingers. Maybe, she thought wryly, this could also act as a dose of self-styled exposure therapy to tone down the way her body reacted to this very real, very physical, man in front of her. She let out a huff of exasperation. *Just wake him and leave, Catarina!* His biceps lay at rest, cast so invitingly over his head. There was nothing inappropriate about touching his arm, right? Her fingers trembled as she reached across and brushed her hand over the bulge of his muscles.

All at once, those muscles came to life. Before Catarina could react, Massimo moved, and she found herself on her back with him over her, pinning her down. She no longer had to wonder about what was under the covers because a long, thick erection was pressed hard between her legs. She let out a moan before she could stop herself.

"*Dio*," he muttered, his voice a husky rasp. "What are you doing?"

Her senses were overloaded with the heat of his body, the scent of him so much more intimate, cologne and something that smelled like pure masculinity.

"I... I..." Catarina struggled to respond, struggled to focus her brain when he was everywhere. But she had gone over her answer too many times to forget it. "I was checking on your concussion. You're not supposed to sleep the full night with a head injury."

For a moment he studied her, as if he was weighing her answer, but then something that could have been dark humor settled in his gaze.

"Are you sure?" he said softly. "If you wanted to see me naked, you just had to ask."

Her entire body was exploding with heat with his words, with his warm, muscular torso pressed against her. Her breaths were coming in short pants, which was only making his case about her intentions stronger.

"I'm talking to a man arrogant enough to try to outrun an avalanche," she muttered. "Of course you would assume I'm here for sex."

"How quickly you jumped from seeing me naked to sex," he said, his voice full of lazy desire. "Interesting."

Embarrassment flashed heat to her cheeks, but Catarina tried her best to glare at him. "Next time I won't bother checking if you are still alive."

"Already planning for next time?" A smile teased at his lips. Then, slowly, Massimo lowered himself onto his elbows, bringing his body to hers. His lips were so close, and she told herself she should resist. Instead, she arched to meet his mouth.

Catarina was everywhere. Her hair spread across the pillow, a backdrop that highlighted her bewitching brown eyes and lush mouth, and her voice rang inside him like a song. Her pert breasts skimmed his chest, and her thighs had parted the moment he had taken control, welcoming him. That scent that emanated from her now was mixed with something blatantly sexual that hijacked every breath of his, urging him to bring his face to her neck and inhale.

This woman was going to be the death of him. He had awakened the moment she entered the room, but had kept still, using his well-honed restraint to put aside temptation and try to discern what she was after. What was her angle? At first, he had assumed she was trying to get the upper hand by crawling into bed with him. That he could have handled.

But instead, as he lowered his mouth to hers, he saw a raw, open longing in her eyes that threatened to take over all rational thought. And before he could weigh whether or not this could still be a complicated game of manipulation, she pressed her lips to his. Massimo groaned as an electric current seemed to arc between them, making every inch of his body come alive. He took his time, tasting her sweet mouth, opening for the soft slide of her tongue as his suspicions faded to the back of his mind.

He wanted this woman. Every inconvenience she had caused him dwarfed in comparison to the want that coursed through him. She shifted, spreading her legs farther, adjusting to fit perfectly under his, and Massimo struggled to keep his sanity as her soft gasps stoked the fire in him higher. The promise of more pleasure was within reach. Just the thinnest scraps of silk separated them from the ecstasy he couldn't stop thinking about. He could have her over and over if he played this right, he reminded himself. If he kept himself under control.

So he forced himself to pull back. Catarina let out a soft whimper that triggered another surge of heat, threatening to overwhelm the thread of control he was hanging on to. He had missed the opportunity to use her desire against her earlier in the day, but now with her below him, the path forward was clear. She wanted pleasure from him, too, making this fire between them a tool. If stoked high enough, a fire had the power to bend even a will of steel, to forge what he ultimately wanted: the convenient fiancée he thought he was getting, who understood the necessity of both their roles in this partnership. Ultimately, he needed a wife who would not, under any circumstances, distract him, preoccupy him or do any of the things that had continued to ruin his father's life and tarnish their family's name. Because even if Catarina was not his mother, he could not ignore the burning need that suggested he was, in fact, at risk of becoming his father.

His cock was notched between her legs, and he flexed his hips experimentally, to see how she reacted. She let out a quiet moan and flexed her own hips, sending a new ripple of pleasure through him. Yes, she definitely craved this.

"Why are you here, Catarina?" He moved more deliberately this time, slowly dragging his cock between her legs, drawing out the pleasure, biting back the drive to finish that was burning in his throat. "Did you come to my room to learn what this feels like? Did you come here so I could show you?"

Massimo did it again and again, moving against her, pressing against that spot that drove her wild. She closed her eyes, as if she was losing herself in the pleasure, and he let her for one more stroke, another, listening as her breaths came faster, turning to soft moans. The music of her voice threatened to overwhelm him, but he resisted. He would not get carried away again. He would stay in control and bring this to the end. He gritted his teeth and dragged his cock against her one last time, then stopped.

Catarina's eyes fluttered open, and she swallowed visibly. Her eyes begged him to continue, and his own body clamored for him to respond. He resisted. He ignored her soft, lush lips, begging to be kissed, and reminded himself of his goal and the promise of future pleasures it brought.

"Answer," he rasped, his voice heavy with the pleasure that threatened to spiral out of control. "Why are you here?"

Her eyes were wide as she blinked up at him, silently begging for more. Though he had told himself he would withhold what she wanted, he moved his iron-hard length between her legs yet another time, and she gasped, as if she was on the edge of ecstasy. As if all it would take to bring her to a climax was one more tilt of his hips. Massimo found that he wanted to give this to her. The drive to please her called from deep inside, casting an ominous shadow over his thoughts.

He waited for her answer, but she didn't reply. Instead, she closed her eyes and moved her hips against his. He glared down at her, telling himself to pull away, but the sound of her gasp held him in place. She moved again and again, using his body to take her own pleasure, testing his sanity until she let out a cry and came apart. A burst of primal satisfaction flooded him as her song of ecstasy threatened to topple the balance that tipped inside him. He fought against the need that pounded inside him. He knew where that path led, and he would not follow it.

CHAPTER SIX

CATARINA HAD ONLY the haziest memory of being carried back to her bed, boneless and still half-delirious from pleasure. The whole encounter was a jumble of dreamlike sensations: the press of Massimo's hard torso on hers; the delicious bliss of his erection between her legs; the rasp of his voice in her ear, taunting, demanding, each word setting off more fireworks inside her. All these came together in an irresistible crescendo too tempting to resist. In the exquisite bliss that followed, he gathered her into his arms with a gentleness that went against everything she knew about him. As she nodded off, clinging to him, the pit of loneliness that sat inside her did not seem as unfathomably deep.

But her memory sharpened the moment Massimo laid her down in her bed. The moment he let go, she looked up at him, silently begging for more, but his expression was an impenetrable mask. Then he was gone. Moments before, she had felt sated, but alone in her bed, the ache inside came back. So quickly and worse than before. In the empty silence of her room she wanted him enough to wake her up after fitful bursts of sleep.

Still, in the light of the morning, Catarina couldn't

bring herself to regret it. Though her late-night adventure had probably made the day in front of her more difficult, the vulnerability quickly faded the moment she realized that, for the first time since her mother's death, she wanted to play the piano. The piano had been the one place in her life where she was allowed free rein to sort out her feelings, a space where she would be left alone because she was using her time "productively."

And then, when her mother died, the music stopped. Every time she sat on the piano bench, a tsunami of grief overtook her. The emotions that had always flowed so freely through her body to her fingertips suddenly buried her in a sea of loss.

But today she had awoken with a giddiness, a feeling that her skin was too small to contain the feelings that were running through her. Quickly, she threw a soft sweater over her silk pajamas and rushed downstairs to the grand piano that shimmered in the bright morning light. Here, she could make sense of these sensations that ran through her. Here, she could get them under control. She opened the lid, bracing herself for five years of grief to wash over her. The grief was still there, hovering, but it didn't cascade onto her the way it had before. Instead, the sensations from the night before came back, punctuated by a burst of hope. Freedom, she told herself. That was what this was; a taste of the long-elusive freedom she had been searching for.

Catarina stared at the keys, suddenly wondering what Massimo would hear as she played. Would he detect these strange layers of old grief and new possibility mixing inside her? Would he know that it was his body, his touch, that had awakened this strange brew of emotions? Everything about this man seemed to be designed to leave her vulnerable. Catarina sat with her back straight and her hands ready, listening to the music that finally played again in her mind and through her body, letting all these thoughts swirl around her.

A creak from the staircase startled her out of this purgatory and into a different one. Catarina swung around, and her heart jumped in her chest. She was entirely unprepared for how it felt to see him again in the clear light of day. He was wearing just a white T-shirt and his perfectly fitted dress slacks that showed off his muscular thighs, the flat planes of his chest and the well-honed contours of his biceps that she had studied so carefully the night before. Massimo had been devastatingly handsome in his white button-down shirt, the sleeves rolled up to expose his corded forearms, just a suggestion of the physical nuances of his body underneath. But the T-shirt put these nuances into sharp focus. Catarina couldn't ignore all the ways Massimo filled out the shirt, stretching at the shoulders and pressing against his hard biceps. In these clothes, the businessman disappeared, leaving just the man, and the bandage that peeked out from behind the silky locks of his hair gave him a rougher appeal.

Her breath caught in her throat. Last night had been so very physical, so very real, and something about that had stripped her layers of protection away, leaving her raw. Vulnerable. She called on her years of practiced distance and found those walls far less sturdy than she remembered.

"Do you play?" Massimo nodded to the piano.

"Not recently."

He tilted his head. "Why?"

This question made her vulnerable in an entirely different way, but she resisted the urge to look away. Powerful men like him were well versed in rooting out people's vulnerabilities as weapons. The best way forward was frank honesty.

"I haven't played since my mother died," she said with a lift of her chin, then braced herself for further prying. He studied her quietly, and his expression softened to what she might, in another man, call gentleness. After a moment, he gave a hint of a nod and asked, "And before that? Did you perform?"

She gave a little laugh. "Only when my parents cajoled me to play a few pieces for guests in our home."

"The first day we met, you said you didn't have a taste for performance."

Catarina was surprised that he had been paying such close attention to what she'd said that day, not between all his orders and demands. A twinge of hope inside her pushed her to continue.

"My father was thrilled at my interest in at least one of the high-value talents that well-bred women of our social standing were supposed to possess," she said wryly. "And my mother encouraged any and all forms of musical interest in hopes that it might lead me closer to a life of performance, the kind she had enjoyed and excelled at. But I've always seen the piano as something for me."

Somehow, the way he was looking at her now felt

just as intimate and dangerous as the unguarded desire in his eyes when she was in his bed, underneath his hard, naked body. This thought was a mistake, because a new jolt of heat ran through her body and made her breaths uneven. Massimo's eyes narrowed with desire.

"I trust you slept well," his deep voice called to her as he came closer, sending a new flash of lust through her.

The inquiry was of the most banal nature. Innocent on the surface, but the wicked quirk of his eyebrow made the bubbling heat inside her rush to her cheeks as she flashed to the memory of the delicious weight of his body over hers as she fell apart in his dark bedroom.

Catarina swallowed and gave him what she hoped was a challenging smile. "Are you looking for praise?"

She felt a surge of satisfaction when his eyes flashed with a mix of surprise and humor. But as he came to a stop next to her, his expression shifted to something both arrogant and sexual.

"I was there, Catarina," he rasped. "I know you enjoyed yourself."

She rolled her eyes, trying to ignore the heat that flashed through her body. "Don't let it go to your head."

He let out a low chuckle. "Are you worried I'm making plans for the next time you show up in my bedroom?"

He said it in that low, seductive voice that suggested he had already thought through said plans. In detail. Her heart pounded in her chest, the way it had the night before. He oozed sensuality, especially when his gaze fixed on her. It was too much. Even under the cover of darkness the night before, she had felt like she was drowning. But in the daylight, there was nowhere to hide when his eyes flashed with undisguised desire. It was like a burst of direct sunlight, and she felt its burn, a warning that suggested the irrevocable harm he could do.

She wanted to create some distance between them, but standing only brought her closer to him. She could simply run away. Part of her wanted to. And yet, something was keeping her in place. Something that kept her there against her will, she told herself. Because wasn't it freedom she was after? And this, right now, felt like the opposite of freedom. So why wasn't she running? Catarina searched for an excuse, for something to say that would break this spell.

"I should get you a change of clothes," she said in a voice that she hoped passed for breezy. "I'll search the Christmas jumper drawer."

Massimo simply looked at her, and she felt his gaze penetrate her, as if he was searching for her vulnerabilities and was on the brink of discovering all of them. He parted his lips, and her first thought was that he was going to kiss her. Instead, he spoke.

"You never answered my question last night, *cara*. Why did you climb into my bed?" His voice was soft and low, coaxing and sensual. A new shiver of desire spread through her. It was simply his physical nearness, she told herself, and the fact that she had never been so close to a man like this, snowbound with no escape. "What do you want?"

This time, the silky veneer of his voice turned into something harder.

And that was enough to shake her out of the haze of desire. She had been taught all her life that it was pointless to take on men like this head-on, that it was better to maneuver, but there was nowhere for her to maneuver. And why wouldn't she simply tell him her purpose? Surely, he had already assumed worse. Maybe a straightforward answer would end this conversation once and for all. She tilted her chin up and said, "I want freedom."

His expression looked thoughtful, and for one short moment, she believed that he had heard her, really heard her and was considering what she said. Her heart soared in her chest, and for that one breathless moment, she believed that there was a way forward, that she could get the freedom she wanted, and that he was not like her father. That despite all the signs to the contrary, he could and would compromise. And she couldn't help that her gaze traveled down to those lips, because if there was hope for compromise, maybe there was hope for even more. Maybe the ache that she had felt all morning was possible to satisfy, too.

But the moment her gaze dipped down to his lips, the pensive expression on his face slowly changed into something else. His eyes narrowed, and his lips took on that twist that couldn't possibly be called a smile. It was something far from humor. It was a warning, but his body was so close that she couldn't bring herself to care.

"The truth, Catarina," he said. "Just the truth."

But there was no time for indignation or outrage or protest, not when his lips brushed against hers.

***

Massimo had wanted to believe her. Her eyes had been so clear when she spoke, and it felt as though the words had come from her whole heart. It would be so much easier if all she wanted was freedom. Of course, only someone never burdened by responsibility truly believed in freedom, but that illusion could fit with his requirements for a marriage of convenience. He had almost been convinced, but then her gaze had dipped to his mouth. That look of carnal desire had flashed in her eyes, a look that had nothing to do with freedom. Massimo knew exactly what it meant. It was a cage he would recognize anywhere, and yet he had been startled to suddenly find himself outside the door of it.

Desire thrummed in his blood. He had waited for this moment since he awoke, and he found his own gaze drawn to her lips, so soft and sensual. He wanted to taste those lips again. He wanted to provoke her, to kiss her until she begged for more. He told himself that this was necessary, a lesson for her and a reminder of how easily he could become a victim of his own desire.

As his eyes dipped to the high flush on her cheeks and the way her full lips parted, as if in anticipation, Massimo thought about the difference that he had seen in her since the first day, the change he had not quite been able to put his finger on. Here, on the mountain, he realized that there was a wildness to her, an untamed part of her that he hadn't seen in Milan. She hid it behind her demure facade, but he had caught more glimpses of it this morning when she sat behind the piano. In this house, surrounded by the endless snow, she was no longer hiding it, and Massimo couldn't shake the feeling this was somehow at the center of why she had fled from him.

But that thought slipped away when she licked her lips. There was nothing between them. There was only the deep brown of her eyes, open and curious, and the bow-shaped mouth that he hungered for. The word *mine* rang through his head, the toll of a bell that called and called in his mind. For once, he did not have to restrain himself from this call. For once, he didn't have to weigh how the decision would affect his business, his family name. Because for once, his wants were in line with his most strategic and expedient move. This moment was born by circumstances that he never would have chosen, but right now, he was no longer angry that she had run because it allowed him to seduce her into granting him the marriage he needed. This moment was a short reprieve from a life of sacrifices. He would take what he craved and give her what she so nakedly asked him for, then hold it up for her to examine.

Slowly, he lowered his head. Her eyes widened, as they had in her kitchen, when he had given in to this urge. Her breath hitched, a sound that shot through him and landed directly in his groin. Purpose faded as he lowered his mouth to hers, lush and red, and he told himself it didn't matter, that this was not the same as giving in to the temptation of her parted lips.

Massimo brought his hands to her flushed cheeks, testing the heat that burned between them. Her skin was soft, and her silky chestnut hair drifted over his hands as Massimo pressed his mouth to hers. The scent of roses overwhelmed him, triggering the memories that had haunted him since the day in their library. Gently, he tasted her again, coaxing her lips open farther until he felt her giving in. He teased her, tilting his mouth for a better angle, and she answered, exploring his mouth tentatively, then with a growing confidence. A surge of satisfaction coursed through him as she came alive under his touch. He fisted her hair and moved his tongue over hers in long, luxurious strokes. With his mouth he promised what he could do with her. For her. He showed her the way that he would please her and she would more than please him.

As he took control of the kiss, she seemed to simply let go, to give in to him. Yes, this was the right way forward. That he could give in to this feeling, just a little bit, just to tempt her further. But soon, his hunger grew stronger, roaring to life. He had it kept tamed so well over the years that he had sometimes even forgotten that it was there. Now it surged, threatening to take over.

Massimo gasped and pulled away. Her mouth was still so tantalizingly close, and she was watching his, but she didn't move closer. She simply stared at him, her eyes both wild and startled, like he was a revelation, and that idea satisfied something inside him. He ignored the warning that clamored because he had her exactly where he wanted her.

"There is no freedom in a kiss like that," he said, letting the wild hunger roughen his voice. She needed to see the dangers of this kind of desire.

Her eyes were bright, and her breaths lifted her chest, pressing against him. "What do you mean?"

"Fires like this burn until they leave everything in ashes." If she did not understand this, she would continue to taunt him with desire. She would tempt him and ruin them both.

At some point, she had reached for him, and her fists were full of his T-shirt. She stared down at her hands for a moment, then let go, smoothing the material with a trembling hand. She took a step back. That hunger inside him roared to life, resisting the distance between them. He had the urge to pull her against him again, but down that road led to disaster, so he gritted his teeth and forced himself to still.

"And we are the future ashes in this scenario?" Catarina sounded more curious than rebuked.

"Not just us," he said gravely.

Massimo watched her carefully as her breaths slowed and her expression returned to that placid, docile mask that somehow provoked a surge of frustration inside him. Because she was proving to be anything but docile.

Massimo flashed to the first moment he saw her this morning, when Catarina sat on the shining black bench of the grand piano, dressed in pajama pants that hinted at the fullness of her thighs and a soft white sweater. Her hair fell over her shoulders in a mass of silken waves that made him ache to weave his hands through it. The keys of the piano were exposed, and sheets of music were arranged in front of her, but her hands were still. On her face was an expression that Massimo could only describe as wild astonishment. He realized with a start that he recognized this expression. She had given him a version of it in her library, and he had written it off as too starry-eyed, full of the unrealistic hopes that he had felt the urge to tame. Just moments ago, when she had given him another version of this same look, he saw something else. He saw dangerous, untamed passion.

But now she wore the mask of the biddable wife again, and Massimo told himself that this was what he wanted. Not the challenge that stoked the fire between them until it threatened to burn out of control.

Catarina tilted her head, as if weighing his words. "Then I suppose that means you shouldn't kiss me anymore. Though that's an interesting take on marriage."

Massimo frowned. "That kiss was a warning that—"

"Yes, yes." She cut him off with a placating smile. "Disaster ahead if we feel passion. I understand."

Massimo stewed over the way she mocked his warning. Clearly, she didn't understand. Which meant that here, in the confines of this home, Massimo needed to demonstrate the danger that lay ahead on this path.

He needed to take her to bed.

It was the answer that his body had begged for ever since she'd entered his room last night, clamoring for attention. But the purpose of taking her to bed was not to satisfy his own needs, he told himself. It was to teach her the lesson that he had learned over and over throughout his life, that passion was a silken noose, so soft and temptingly sensual, that slowly slipped tighter and tighter until it suffocated. Better to teach this lesson now, when they were stuck here together, so she would learn it quickly instead of drawing it out over the years.

"But you still want to play with this fire?" he asked softly. Another warning.

"Are you trying to protect me from myself?" She looked almost...amused. "How sweet."

Before he could answer, she walked away.

Massimo stared out the window at the thick wall of snow that held them here, trying to tame the frustration and desire that brewed inside him. *Dio*, this woman was driving him crazy. He wanted her in a way that defied rational thought. But he had controlled this want, he reminded himself, and he would continue to keep himself in line. But wasn't his whole life's work perfectly suited to this task? From the moment he and Alessandro had taken over the family's company, he had learned to put his own needs aside to lead others down a path that, in the end, was ultimately to his benefit. He had done it in far more high-stakes conditions, he told himself, and yet there was a dark rumbling inside that told him that never had the stakes been higher. But he would master this control. And if she refused to respond in an acceptable way? Massimo could end their marriage arrangement and find a more biddable bride. The idea turned over inside him uncomfortably. In fact, he found that even thinking about this option provoked a strong distaste.

No. He would make this arrangement work. And it *would* work as long as he didn't mistake his own lust for anything more than a tool to be wielded carefully and precisely, a tool to help negotiate a marriage that would show the world that, contrary to his father's example, Carandini marriages were a stabilizing force in the dynasty. Emilio Carandini was the colorful exception, not the rule. The problem wasn't the family's temperament, as some tabloids had suggested when Massimo and Alessandro were kicked out of school. Massimo Carandini was not his father, as he had reminded himself so many times, and he never would be. Though less attraction between them would be ideal, if she could master it, they could craft an acceptable form of marriage. Every bit of his investigation suggested she knew how to calculate her best interests. Tonight he would nudge her to apply this skill to their relationship.

Catarina d'Avalos was sheltered, her visions of marriage no doubt as fanciful as those in the books that lined her extensive library shelves. She had made it clear that she'd wanted a bit of romance, and though this was far outside his natural inclination, Massimo had a few ideas to work with at the moment. The fire that sparked between them had made her curious, so he would flame it.

He would spend time softening her, opening her for seduction, which eventually could make her pliable, amenable to his will. To make this work, he would likely need to be more approachable, less intensely… himself. Temporarily, of course, until she agreed to the marriage bargain. Strangely, he felt an unfamiliar hesitancy with the ruthlessness of his plan of using her softness, her curiosity, against her. He felt a confounding aversion to the idea of taking advantage of her vulnerability. After all, he had chosen her precisely for these characteristics. But he pushed this hesitation away. He would simply get what he wanted from her, so they could come to an understanding that she could soon realize suited them both. And then he would move on from this distraction. They would live separate lives the way the most levelheaded members of society did, coming together occasionally only to slake any lingering desire. Children would, of course, put them in closer proximity, as he had no intention of neglecting his children the way his parents had. But that was a problem for long in the future. For now, he would draw her out with passion and bring her back to those first moments in the library, when she had been prepared to marry him.

CHAPTER SEVEN

AFTER A DAY of slinking around, trying to avoid Massimo *in her own house*, Catarina gave up. Her breaking point was the scent of garlic, olive oil and spices that seeped under her door and swirled in the air. Was Massimo...cooking? It was an image she couldn't quite conjure in her mind, and yet, as she rounded the corner to the kitchen, she found Massimo in front of the oven looking as if he belonged there. He was wearing a new T-shirt that fit in all the right places, and the sweatpants sat temptingly low on his hips. In one hand he held a dish with an oven mitt, and with the other, he squeezed a lemon in his large, capable hand. Dark, wavy locks of hair hung over his forehead as he worked, obscuring the bandaged cut. Catarina found her gaze pulled back to the way the muscles on his forearm flexed as he held the pan. He looked focused on the task in front of him, shockingly at home in the kitchen in a way that she herself had never been. The scene was captivating.

Catarina didn't realize he was aware of her presence until he turned and gave her a smile dazzling enough to momentarily stun her. "I hope you're hungry."

"I thought Alessandro was the charming one," she

said. "Did you do some sort of twin switch with your brother?"

"I contain multitudes of layers, Catarina." He said it with his usual self-important seriousness, but followed the statement with a wry smile. Was he laughing at his own intensity level? "I hope you like fish."

"Much better than my plan for shrimp, mayonnaise, dill and cucumber sandwiches."

He arched an eyebrow. "Interesting choice."

His tone suggested he was glad he knew how to cook.

"It's a Norwegian tradition that reminds me of summer." Summers with her mother.

He nodded. "Then that's understandable."

"How gracious of you to say so," she said with mock sincerity. "The country is grateful for your approval."

His eyes danced with humor, and she had the same off-kilter feeling she'd had a moment before. He was so much more approachable all of a sudden, as if he wanted to please her. This was enough of a change to make her suspicious. Or maybe she was just irritated by the fact that he had taken over her kitchen.

"Please…" he said, then gestured to the table.

"Make myself at home?" She flashed him a wry smile. "Thank you."

Catarina turned to the dining room area and noted what she had somehow missed in her dazed walk from the stairs to the kitchen: The table had been transformed. Massimo had pulled out one of the many linens her grandmother had monogrammed and laid it across the far side of the long table, creating a more intimate space. On it, he had placed candles at the center that he had gathered from various shelves. Two places were set, facing each other, using her grandmother's silver, and to the side of the candles was a chilling bucket for wine. Catarina eyed the platter of olives, figs, olive-oil-soaked goat cheese and a selection of crisp crackers, some of which she didn't even know she had, and she wanted to make another comment along the lines of making himself at home, but the voice stuck in her throat. The table was beautiful, and he had somehow transformed the emptiness of this house, with its ghost that still lingered, into something inviting. She approached the table and sat in one of the tall-backed chairs where her former life had played out, bracing herself for the familiar rush of sadness. But instead, Catarina felt a small burst of something else. Was it hope?

The thought made her want to retreat to her room, and maybe she would have if she hadn't been so incredibly hungry and if the scent of the food he had prepared hadn't been so intoxicating. *That's not the only reason*, said a voice somewhere deep inside. She felt Massimo behind her, stirring the heat that seemed to grow stronger each time he was near.

"I hope you approve," he said.

"It's lovely," she acknowledged softly, hoping her voice didn't betray a hint of the wistfulness she was trying to tamp down.

But Massimo's words from her father's library returned, mocking this optimism. *I was given to understand that you were clear about the nature of our agreement*. She absolutely shouldn't pin hopes on this man. He had made that perfectly clear.

He set another plate on the table, this one a grilled antipasto platter of zucchini, carrots and red onions with a creamy dip that gave off hints of garlic. She had been entranced by this man from the moment she walked toward him in the family library. His raw sexuality was overwhelming. But this Massimo Carandini, who'd created a multi-course meal from the ingredients Signe had brought and no recipe? He was even more dangerous. This softer, more approachable man intrigued her, even when she knew better than to trust his motivations. And underneath it all was still the thrum of their electric connection that sparked and sizzled inside her.

Catarina took a long breath. The kiss this morning had been a lesson, probably even a warning of what lay ahead. That he had meant it as such had been clear. Was he right that there was no room for freedom in a kiss like theirs? It certainly wasn't freedom she had felt when she'd clung to his shirt as if it was a life raft in the storm of their kiss. She knew cages, and this didn't feel like one. It was something new, something that she needed to understand, especially if she were to marry Massimo.

Was she still considering this marriage? When she fled to this mountain refuge, all she could think about was escape—from her father, from the marriage, from Massimo. She had put aside the feeling in the library and left, and maybe she could have hardened her resolve if he hadn't followed her. But now she knew the way it felt when his stern gaze darkened with desire, when his solid frame pressed against hers, his soft lips coaxing hers open, his hard length between her legs, the intent unmistakable. Everything about him preoccupied her to the point of distraction. Maybe she could make sense of this feeling that giving in to her desire for Massimo could cost her everything. It was their situation, this inescapable closeness, she told herself, that sparked this intense flame between them.

Through the windows, the snow continued to fall. The light from the candles reflected on the walls and warmed the hue of Massimo's bronze skin as he opened the bottle of wine and poured her a glass. He took his seat across from her and raised his. "To unexpected pleasures."

She raised her glass and smiled. "Pleasures like avalanches and head injuries?"

"My head is fine, but thank you for your...concern last night." His eyes darkened, as if he was remembering the scene.

Her face flushed, but she gave him a mild smile. "I think the bare minimum of my host duty is to make sure my guest doesn't lose consciousness."

His laugh was deep and sensual. "You can consider your duty well-done."

"I'll take that as glowing praise," she said primly, but as embarrassment heated her cheeks, she found herself smiling, too.

As Catarina took a sip of her wine, she studied Massimo, aware that he wanted something from her, even demanded it from her at their first meeting. That day, the demand had felt too much like obedience for her to ignore it. Was he trying a softer tactic to the same end, or was this softness an opening to another possibility between them?

Explore it, her body begged traitorously, so willing to ignore the wariness this implacable man stirred inside her. Or maybe this flutter in her stomach was something far more tempting than wariness. Maybe this was why her father had kept her hidden away, she thought darkly. Because Giuseppe d'Avalos knew the power that one person could hold over another. He lived with the loss of it every day. Had he arranged this marriage to help her avoid the same kind of devastation? The idea was a revelation. She could see the merits of this approach, but it was not possible with Massimo. Not when it felt as if he was a gravitational force, and she was helpless to resist the pull.

The table gave her a little space, enough to remind herself that she, too, could play Massimo's game. She could use this situation to better understand this man who was determined enough to pursue her that he'd ignored avalanche conditions. Despite the fact that he had shown so little interest in her own wants and needs back in Milan. In his bed last night he had shown a completely different side of himself, and now he had prepared a meal for her. At the very least, a little prying could help her make a decision about their future.

"Have you visited Norway before?" she asked.

"I have stayed in Oslo for business, but I have never seen this." His large hand indicated the windows that lined the room, all clouded in endless snow.

"Impressive, isn't it?"

Massimo looked out into the white abyss, and she

wondered if he was contemplating the storm that had the power to bring even him to a halt? When he turned back to her, he gave a subtle nod in assent and took a drink of his wine.

"But I imagine you've traveled to plenty of other far-flung places," she said.

"My travel is almost exclusively to cities for work."

"But as a child…?"

"When my parents traveled, Alessandro and I did not come." There was a flicker of a frown on his lips when he mentioned his parents, but he smoothed it over with a smile. "Though a few of our boarding schools could qualify as far-flung."

"In Italy?"

"The far-flung schools were in Switzerland, but the last one we attended was in Milan." He chuckled. "Our grandparents wanted to keep a closer eye on us."

Catarina was intrigued by this emerging sketch of Massimo's background. Multiple boarding schools suggested a teen who exercised far less of his current iron control.

"It must have been a comfort to have your brother with you," she said a little wistfully, thinking back to that strange feeling of isolation at a new school.

Massimo laughed. "Alessandro was often more trouble than comfort."

And yet, the warmth in his voice suggested a closeness to his brother.

"All those years at boarding school, and yet you cook? I must say it's a little unexpected," she said. "Even for a man of all your accomplishments."

Massimo flashed her a devastatingly handsome smile, threatening her last defenses. "You may want to reserve your praise until after you try it."

She gestured to the bandage on his forehead, just barely visible under his thick locks of hair. "I have heard many strange reports of survivors of car crashes, people speaking with ghosts or waking up with full novels in their head that they had to write down. But I have never heard of a crash that left someone with professional-level cooking skills. Truly, it's a miracle."

Massimo's stark features lightened, and he laughed, his eyes crinkling in the corners in a way that made her heart stutter. He had been called a lot of things in the press—driven, obstinate, demanding—and their first meeting had more than confirmed those descriptions. But right now, Massimo looked almost…at ease. She was wary of the way she felt herself softening toward him.

"I am afraid the explanation is rather prosaic," he said, the humor still dancing in his voice. "My grandparents did not grow up wealthy. When my grandmother saw the direction my father was taking the business, she decided to arm her grandchildren with more practical skills."

"How very sensible of her," she said. "I wish I could give her my compliments."

"She would be delighted to know her efforts were not wasted," he said, though Catarina doubted his grandmother had worried about Massimo's determination to master whatever the lesson had been. Even in the little time Catarina had known him, she had gleaned that anything that Massimo did, he would relentlessly pursue excellence.

Massimo looked out the window and added, "Her lessons have proved useful in many ways."

"Indeed. My father tells me that you and your brother rebuilt your family's business from the ground up."

"We had the Carandini name to redeem. It was our duty," he said with a mixture of pride and self-deprecating humor.

Massimo was the third-generation holder of the Carandini family legacy, and though his father had done plenty to ruin it, he and his brother had so quickly and thoroughly rebuilt it. It was why Catarina was being offered up to him, the prize her father so readily turned over: because he would protect her with his name. Marrying into this family would ensure her future. And yet, she sensed that his efforts were about more than a duty to the Carandini name.

She couldn't help but notice that when he laughed, he looked almost…younger, like a different person, one who had been taken away at birth and lived a much more comfortable life. It was a strange thought.

She lifted her glass and met his gaze, and she could feel the humor in his eyes shift into something different, something that stirred the want bubbling inside her.

"Your mother's death must have been difficult," he said, watching her carefully. "I saw the photo of the two of you together in my room."

She looked away. Her pain was something private, something that no one, not even her father, could understand. And yet, she felt strangely soothed by his tone. "It was. I traveled with her quite a bit. My father occasionally met up with us, but often it was just my mother and me."

"I'm sorry," he said softly.

"Thank you," she said, taking a drink of her wine, busying herself with anything besides meeting his gaze. She didn't want him to see the rawness in this topic. Still, after four years.

In many ways, the man across from her was who she had hoped to find when Massimo had walked into the library. That day, she had decided that man was an illusion, a figment of her imagination. But today, in the glow of the candlelight, she felt the tempting stirrings of hope.

She took a bite of the exquisite fish, decorated with herbs and lemons and asked, "Where does your grandmother live?"

"In her country home in the mountains near Lake Como, though she still stays in Milan from time to time."

"And this country home is where you learned to cook?"

"Among other skills," he said. Then his gaze turned darker. "Neither of my parents could be called anything close to practical, but my grandparents enjoyed running an estate of that size, even as their health declined. My grandfather passed away a few years ago, but running the estate is still a part of my grandmother's daily life. They want Alessandro or me to take it over someday."

He took a drink of his wine and continued. "When the two of us were kicked out of our boarding school in Montreux and our parents were away on one of their many reconciliation vacations to Seychelles, we were shipped back to Lake Como. Our grandparents decided that a practical connection to the world was in order. They felt that they had spoiled and corrupted their only son, and they were determined not to let the same happen to the two of us. The result is that I can cook and tend to animals and an orchard, build fences and make fires, to name a few. In retrospect, that summer was the happiest of my childhood."

There was a warning in his tone that told her not to ask more, but she ignored it. This was her chance to learn about him.

"I would not have guessed that you were the type to be kicked out of school," she mused. "Though you did mention trouble with Alessandro…"

"I took away a lot from the experience that summer, including that serious, hard work soothed a lot of my anger," he said. Then, unexpectedly, he laughed. "My brother seemed to have taken an entirely different lesson from it."

Alessandro Carandini was as well-known as Massimo, which was why her father would never have considered him as a candidate for marriage. He was, in crass terms, a playboy, someone with a charm that had drawn in princesses and commoners alike. But none of his attachments lasted for longer than a few weeks. Massimo's reputation was the opposite of charm, though she was starting to understand that he was perfectly capable of it. Instead, he seemed to have made a deliberate decision not to use it.

But she was listening closely to the tone that Massimo's voice had taken when he doled out these little hints of his background. He loved his grandmother, that much was clear, and maybe Catarina had expected that, but what she hadn't expected was the depth of emotion she could hear he had for his brother. If one were to read the tabloids, one might assume that the two brothers were at odds, their warring personalities pulling them in different directions.

But most notable was the icy bite he reserved for his parents and the warning she sensed as he moved the conversation away from the topic. She knew the basics of his parents' very public excesses, but now she wished she had probed further at these stories. She wanted to ask more but was almost sure her questions would be shut down. She needed to take a subtle approach.

Catarina had intended to quickly eat and then withdraw to her suite, but he was keeping her here, not with coercion but with the intensity that seemed to radiate from him, sprinkled with unexpected humor. At times, his eyes sparkled with amusement as he spoke, but under his smile she felt there was something carnal lurking, something her body seemed particularly attuned to. Those moments reverberated inside her, leaving a tingling sensation running through her limbs.

As the white landscape darkened, she could feel the lure of this man across from her grow stronger. But if she were to marry him, she needed more, she reminded herself. Would he lower his guard for her even further? It was hard to be strategic when she wanted to run her hands through the silky waves of his hair. To trace the sharp angles of his cheekbones, of his jaw, the hard planes of his chest that had tempted her the night before.

She reminded herself that Massimo had arrived so unceremoniously at the bottom of her driveway determined to take her back to Milan. He had been so sure he could bend her to his will and make her do something she didn't want to do, and the only thing that stopped his plan was a literal force of nature. Catarina knew she was still the bird in this arrangement and Massimo held the cage. Even if he gave her the illusion of flying right now, he could just as easily show her the bars, gilded or ironclad. Not once had he *asked* about what she wanted, which suggested that either he hadn't considered this angle or he didn't care. She wasn't sure which was worse.

That first day, he had shattered her imaginings of him as a sort of fairy-tale prince, someone she had seen across the room and projected her own ideas and dreams onto. Why had she been surprised when he made it so unmistakably clear that he was not the person she had invented on that first day? And yet, despite the fact that she knew better, Catarina could feel her dreams come to life again. This conversation was a glimpse beneath his harder exterior to a man vulnerable and hurt by the past in a way that resonated deep inside her. She had no idea what to do about it.

But whether or not she chose to marry Massimo, she knew she wanted him. She wanted to know what it was like to give in to the desire that had been building all day, just to see what it felt like to be free to follow what her body begged her to do. All day, she had told herself that the growing want inside was simply physical attraction and curiosity, natural for someone with as little experience as she had but also something easily disrupted with distance. But as she watched Massimo across the table, she had the growing suspicion that this feeling inside was more complicated.

It felt like music.

Every comment was a prelude to something distinctly intimate, each exchange a crescendo. But unlike the scores that she had listened to and played countless times, this piece was unwritten. She could not simply choose an etude from the shelf, depending on her mood. She could not use a concerto to invite particular feelings to wash over her and then let them come to their predictable end. This time, she had no idea where the music would lead her. She had no idea which emotions it would expose, and there was no way to preview the score before she sat down on the bench to gauge whether the piece suited her. Too late, she found that this concerto was playing faster than she could keep up with and, too late, she was realizing that this was no longer her score alone to play. It was Massimo's, too. She felt the crescendo between them growing. *Give in*, it sang. *Give in.*

Maybe she would. As long as she remembered not to mistake the desire that reverberated inside her for anything more.

He found Catarina far too intriguing. Her dark eyes were so soft as she'd listened to stories about his family, and there was empathy in her voice when she responded. That was the only explanation for why he found himself offering too many details about the past he had worked so hard to leave behind. It was the only explanation for the overwhelming need to know more about her, to understand her. The knowledge was strategic, he told himself to calm the unease stirring inside. These were details he could leverage to craft their marriage.

"What would make you happy, Catarina?" This was a different version of the question that he had thrown at her since he'd set foot in this house, a question she had dodged and answered with what he was certain were half-truths. But this version seemed to get through. Her eyes widened in surprise, and then she tilted her head, as if she was truly considering it.

"For a long time, I thought the only thing that would make me happy was if my mother was alive. Not possible, of course, but that's what I wanted. And I still want that." Her voice wavered at those last words, and something twisted in his gut. "I want children, though maybe not right away. But my family has always been at the center of my life, and I cannot imagine it otherwise."

She paused and looked away.

"I was being honest when I told you I wanted freedom," she continued, her voice steadier. "In hindsight, I can see I lived a very sheltered life under my mother's wing, and life was easier that way. But I don't want to go back to that. I want to discover what is meaningful to me. That's what I meant by freedom."

"You deserve to have this." His words came out more forcefully than he'd intended.

Catarina's laugh lacked the humor that had laced their conversation until the topic turned to her. "Few people in this world get what they deserve."

Massimo found that he didn't like this answer. Right now, she looked so lovely, so self-contained, as if she could weather any storm gracefully, and Massimo told himself that this was exactly why he had chosen her. And yet, the idea that she viewed her own life through this lens was…dissatisfying.

"But there must be things you've dreamed of doing," he pressed.

"When I was young, my parents and I watched a movie with scenes in a hospital, and after this, I declared that I wanted to be a nurse," she said. "Of course, my father laughed, and said, you will have plenty of opportunities to take care of someone. And now, here we are."

She glanced at the bandage on his head. Her voice held that light, airy tone, but he couldn't miss the undertones of irony.

"Is that the university path you were referring to when we were in the library?" he asked.

She raised her eyebrow, and he got the sense that she was surprised he remembered this piece of information. Then she waved off his comment.

"That whim has come and gone," she said lightly. "Those are not the kinds of skills I was taught at boarding school, though my mother and I did go through CPR and first aid training. My father insisted when we began traveling alone. I'm so glad to have the opportunity to put these skills to use."

There was a flicker of emotion in her eyes, and then it was gone.

"I supposed you could always pursue a career in top secret witness extraction or the like," he said.

Catarina blinked at him, then did the most unexpected thing. She laughed. Nothing had prepared him for the sound of her laugh, musical and intimate. He could hear that it was a real laugh, one that slipped from behind the polite mask that she wore so diligently. It was a laugh just for him. Even more improbably, he felt the corners of his own mouth tug up in answering humor.

She shook her head. "You didn't have to work too hard to find me. Thanks to my father's guidance, of course."

It wasn't bitterness in her voice but something that sounded like betrayal. He discovered he did not like that sound.

"I would have found you anywhere." His smile faded as much baser feelings surged through him.

Her eyes flared with heat, and she stood suddenly. He rose and circled the table. Her breath caught. She was close enough to touch, and he needed to be closer. He wanted to lean forward and press his mouth against the slim column of her neck, to the hollow where her heartbeat raced. She stared up at him with those wide eyes, and those beautiful red lips parted, waiting for his. He tottered on the precipice of control. He wanted to take her right there on the table, so driven with this disturbing need to make her his. Because he wanted her. He needed her like he needed his next breath.

Under no circumstances could Massimo lose control. He could not lose sight of the seduction as a path to marriage. Catarina was an innocent, and she wanted more than a man who could not and would not ever give her the love she deserved. *Deserved.* He had no idea where that thought came from, but the words rang in his head, and he took them as the warning that they were.

So he resisted every urge inside him and stepped back, leaving her room to pass. His own retreat shocked him, right at the moment he was getting what he wanted. It was strategic, he told himself, even if the thoughts of what she deserved echoed ominously inside him. Catarina paused, her eyes searching his, maybe even pleading. Then she looked away and left him standing alone in the room.

As her footsteps on the staircase echoed in the room, Massimo drank the last of his wine, focusing on its cool trail down his throat, forcing his thoughts to the crisp floral notes of the Vernaccia di San Gimignano, reminding himself that his driving desire for this woman did not rule him. Reminding himself that this seduction was a calculated risk, that any end game had winners and losers. And he never intended to find himself in the latter category.

The rational choice was to back out of their marriage deal altogether, to weather this runaway fiancée scandal to avoid the risk of a much larger one, a scandal born in this weakness that had the power to lead him down the same path as his father. And yet, Massimo knew he was not going to let her go.

Until they returned to Milan, he would focus on

securing this marriage. He would highlight the kinds of sensual promises he could give her. These promises weren't a lie, he told himself. Not exactly. In the future, he would need to slake this burning thirst for her from time to time. But he would limit their interactions when they returned to Milan, of course, until this dangerous urge to possess her wholly was under control. At that point, far, far in the future, they could negotiate children.

For now, he would satisfy the need that sparked between them, both his and hers. Tonight he would give her the passion she craved. Though this spark between them threatened to flare out of control each time she was close, experience told him that it would eventually fade, most often sooner rather than later. And any power she held over him would be lost.

But this remote fjord felt so far away from his business and the weight of his family name. It seemed to whittle his thoughts down to something baser, something much more compelling. For now, his next move was not to subdue this fire. His next move was to show her all the ways to stoke it higher.

Massimo slowly made his way across the great room. He was in control. He focused on the most efficient, expedient route to his goal. He headed for his room and searched his wallet for a condom, shoving it into his pocket. Then he strode to the opposite end of the hallway and entered her bedroom.

The lights were off, but moonlight echoed off the snow and through the window, casting a dreamlike glow over the room. Her bedroom's design was much like the rest of the house, with vaulted ceilings, exposed beams and plush carpets scattered over the wooden floors, but this room had a more feminine twist. Clouds of pillows were scattered over a puffy down duvet, and the wooden dresser and mirror were carved with flourishes. Matching bookcases lined the other side of the room, and he wondered what books she held here in her private library. But that thought faded as his gaze drifted to the window. Catarina stood next to a reading chair, and the long shadow of her profile cast a graceful image across the floor. She was dressed in a long gown that covered her form, and yet it was made of a material that the moonlight rendered translucent. It highlighted her soft, rounded thighs, the generous swell of her rear, the tight buds of her breasts. Massimo hardened as he traced each curve with his gaze. Catarina turned, looking over her shoulder at him, and he couldn't decide if he had startled her or if she had been expecting him. Maybe it was both.

His fingers ached to trace each curve, to feel the weight of her full breasts, to tease the hardness of her nipple, and his groin throbbed, begging him to do it. *You can give in just this once*, he reminded himself, just to show her what this could be like. Somewhere in the back of his mind, he registered that this need for Catarina complicated their situation. She would be an indulgence, one he would strictly limit before the siren call of attraction grew too strong. But by then she would be his forever. Or maybe it was the reverse. Maybe it was he who would be hers. But Massimo was long past caring.

He didn't remember deciding to move, and yet he was crossing the room. She said nothing, just watched him. He stopped in front of her, close enough that her warm breaths brushed over his skin, close enough to see the plea in her eyes, both pushing him away and calling him closer. The lure was irresistible.

"Surrender," he rasped, and the words were as much a promise to himself as they were a plea to her. "Surrender to this."

CHAPTER EIGHT

Catarina blinked up at the man in front of her, letting his features come into focus. The moonlight highlighted the contrasts on the sharp planes of his cheekbones, bringing the harsh angle of his jaw into relief. His brown eyes were obscured in the darkness, but she could see his mouth—a harsh, grim line. Tension radiated from his body in hot waves. Yesterday she might have mistaken these signs for anger. Maybe there was some of that, too, but today she understood he wanted her. Perhaps it was because she was also thrumming with a need that wound her up and begged for release, but there was no mistaking his intent, despite her innocence. Her body knew. *Surrender.* The word whispered through her, echoing in his deep rumble of a voice that created friction inside her, one she was desperate to soothe.

After reasoning through this all day, debating whether she should give in to this need, right now she could see that reasoning was irrelevant. With him so near, the lure of his sensuality was too powerful to resist. *Surrender.* Whatever else happened between them, at least this experience would be hers.

Slowly, she lifted her hand to his face. The brush of scruff on his chin scraped her tender skin, adding another sensation to this cauldron that was bubbling inside her, a tonic that felt almost otherworldly. Massimo let out a groan, and then the tension in him seemed to snap. His mouth came down on hers for a devastating kiss that was nothing like the one earlier in the day. That kiss had been a slow seduction, a temptation. This one was lush and indulgent and greedy. It was everything she had spent a lifetime training herself never to be. And yet, here with his heat and his masculine scent surrounding hers, she finally let go.

Catarina explored his mouth without shame, took without worrying about giving, but every one of her sighs was matched by his groans, louder and deeper. Massimo was taking what he wanted, too. His hands found her hips, then moved up her body, the whisper-thin material of her nightgown brushing over her skin, so deliciously sensual, setting her insides on fire. He angled his mouth and took their kiss deeper, and she found herself gasping for air, trying to get enough, trying to get closer. She pressed her body against his and felt his hard length, so solid and so *there*, a stark, tempting reminder of what could come next. And oh, how she wanted it. Underneath all her dreams and fairy-tale endings lay something so breathtakingly raw, something she had never imagined and yet somehow, her body still knew she had wanted it the whole time.

Massimo pulled away from the kiss and swore under his breath. The lines on his face were so harsh that, for a moment, he looked almost angry. But then all thoughts left her because he was kissing her again, taking with a hunger that made her weak and sending pulses of need between her legs. She grabbed onto the hard muscles of his shoulders, steadying herself.

His kisses traveled down her neck, over her chest, and then he cupped one of her breasts. His mouth covered it, and she drew in a frantic breath as pleasure burst through her. Before she had time to recover, he sucked on her nipple, and it was as if there was a direct line from her breast to the sensitive bud at her core. Her insides burned and her legs ached as his tongue circled, coaxing. The room echoed with cries, and she was suddenly aware that they were coming from her. She was losing all control.

Massimo lifted her, and in a few quick steps her back was against the wall. One thick forearm held her against him so that her core rested on one of his hard thighs, and between his legs, her own thigh was pressed against his long, insistent length. Cool air drifted over the wet material of her gown, pressing against her nipple, bringing a shiver of pleasure through her whole body. Massimo swore again, then took her other breast in his mouth and, with a shift of his large hand, rubbed the bud between her legs against his thigh. It was too much. She came apart in a spectacular crescendo of pleasure, her cry hoarse as she shuddered and shook. If he hadn't been holding her so firmly, she would've collapsed, but he held her body snugly between him and the wall as she simply let go, let the waves of pleasure wash over her.

His breaths were rasps in her ear as he lifted her, his

soft touch against her back so at odds with the harsh look she had glimpsed on his face and the thick, insistent pulse of his steely length against her thigh. He carried her over to the bed and gently set her there. Her nightgown was askew, and Massimo was staring at her with a look that could only be described as thunderous. He took a step back, and a whiff of panic startled her out of this languid purgatory of pleasure. He was going to leave. She was sure of it.

"Don't go." She meant it as a plea, but her voice was an invitation filled with pleasure.

He swore again. Massimo Carandini, who had bent the entire world to his will, wanted her. The thought was a powerful aphrodisiac that sparked new desire inside her, opening her curiosity. If he could bring so much delicious pleasure with just his mouth on her breasts and his thigh between her legs, what would happen when he used more? The *more* in question was on display, straining against the material of his sweatpants. She ached to explore it.

"Surrender," she whispered, echoing his word that was still ringing in her head; the word that had brought her to this point of uncharted pleasure.

Massimo closed his eyes, and he shuddered. Then he grasped for the hem of his T-shirt and pulled it off, exposing the hard muscles she had thought about all day. But nothing in her imagination could have prepared her for the way they moved with each of his breaths. It was clear that he was no stranger to physical work. She had felt his hard biceps as he held her, and she could see the ripples of strength across his chest. In front of her were the ridges of his abs and the trail of hair that disappeared into his waistband, so close and on blatant display. She wanted to get on her knees to explore him, but before she could even think to move, he was stripping off the sweatpants and his boxers, and then he was naked in front of her, his erection proud and so much larger than she had imagined.

"Stand up. I want you closer."

His voice was gentle, almost tender, and she responded to it immediately. He closed the distance between them and lifted her nightgown until she was naked, too. And whatever had been satisfied inside her just moments before turned back to want. This want felt so much larger, so much more overwhelming because he was now bare before her, and somehow, the promise of pleasure for both of them made it even stronger. Catarina reached for his chest and touched him tentatively, and she felt his muscles tighten under her hand. He let out a sound too raw to be called a laugh.

"Careful." The word echoed with an unmistakable warning.

But Catarina was done being careful. She was done being the person her father wanted, and she had long been cast out from the sheltered life that revolved around her mother. Every moment, every move, was now hers. Though she had no idea how this would play out, she knew she wanted it. So she slid her hand up his chest, feeling the thump of his heart, relishing in his desperate breaths and the electric power of touching his skin.

Just a man, she reminded herself, but she found this

was no longer a comfort, now that she had had a taste of what this man could do with her. To her. Catarina explored, and he stood still, letting her, using his well-known control. Except this control seemed to be teetering on the edge of something else, something she wanted desperately to understand. A rush of satisfaction surged through her. *She* had this effect on him. But as she moved her hand lower, to the trail of hair on his stomach, he grabbed her wrist. Before she could register what was happening, he cleared the bed of her billowy duvet and pillow with his other hand, and then she was on it. He leaned down for something, and she heard the rip of a package. A condom. He rolled it down his length, and she watched, entranced. He climbed on top of her, nudging her thighs open, and settled there so easily that it felt as though his body had been made for hers. He propped himself on his elbows, his body skimming over hers, his muscles flexing under his weight, and his hardness, thick and full against her core, moving over it with delicious friction, setting off a fresh wave of pleasure. He didn't seem to notice any of that. He was staring at her face.

"Surrender," he said in a voice so stark, so final, that at once she could feel that he was not simply asking for sex. He was demanding something much more devastating.

Then, the nudge of his hardness pressed against her, and all other thoughts disappeared.

Holding himself on the brink of ecstasy, Massimo stared down at Catarina. Her thick brown hair spread over the pillowcase in waves, her lush lips were parted and her eyes were innocent and wide, as if she was on the verge of a discovery so unexpected, so earth-shattering, that she didn't know what to do.

But Massimo knew exactly what to do. He knew what she needed because he felt that same need pulsing through his own body. He was no longer going to lie to himself, not after seeing her response to his touch; not after tasting those tight buds of her nipples in his mouth; not after the way she drove him wild with her cries. He needed this like he needed his next breath. All the havoc that this feeling could wreak on his life he would contemplate later, but now was the time to answer this siren's call. To surrender to it. Both of them.

He stroked himself along her soft core one more time, gritting his teeth against the overwhelming urge to let go, instead focusing on the hitch of her breath, the moans and sighs that sent rushes of pleasure through him. Then he positioned himself at her entrance and nudged in, straining at the tight fit, slowly easing himself into the hot, welcoming place he craved. His desire spiked higher with each of her breaths. She was so soft and wet from her pleasure that when he came to the point of resistance, he almost forgot to stop. He almost lost control.

But suddenly, her muscles tensed, jolting him back from the edge of ecstasy. He felt a resistance, and wariness now clouded her eyes.

"I'll take care of you," he whispered, stroking his hand over the silky skin of her cheek. "I promise."

He had meant to comfort her, but her eyes inexplicably filled with tears. He froze, then pulled back, searching her gaze for what had gone wrong. But she shook her head and pulled him closer.

"Please," she said in a voice that was husky with need. "I want this."

I want you. Satisfaction soared through him. It should have been satisfaction that his seduction plan had worked, but the pleasure that ran through him was complicated in a way that he couldn't begin to contemplate. So he didn't. He lowered himself to kiss her, pressing his mouth to hers, and that magical thing that seemed to happen each time her lips touched his happened again. He lost himself in the kiss as he slowly, slowly, continued to push. He felt the moment where the resistance gave, felt her flinch. He soothed her with more kisses until she moved, urging him deeper and deeper until finally, *finally*, he was inside her completely.

"*Catarina.*" Her name slipped out of his mouth, his voice a rasp of insatiable hunger that lurked inside him. As sensations threatened to overwhelm him, a sudden thought darkened the bliss of that moment: This was something he would never come back from. The idea swirled inside him, an uncomfortable mix of fear and satisfaction that he tried to push away. Then she moved again, and he moved, too, focusing on reining in his control, pleasuring her, holding himself on the edge of abyss. Each stroke, each cry, took him further into pleasure, building it until the whole world fell away, and it was only this connection between them. With another hard thrust she fell apart in his arms, shuddering with cries that broke him. He came with a long, guttural groan that reverberated through his entire body. Ecstasy flooded him in wave after wave as her body responded, drawing out both their pleasure. He held himself over her, his lips pressed to her neck, breathing in her scent, until the world took shape again.

He rolled onto his side, bringing her with him, and she held on to him with an intensity that was almost too much to bear. The small gasps of her breaths echoed through the quiet room, in this house so far away from the ceaseless demands of his life. But for once, he just let the weight of history and the future be. He stayed inside her as the sharp ecstasy of pleasure turned into something warmer, something fuller. She was his now in a way that reached beyond business deals and marriage contracts. The thought gave him a surge of visceral satisfaction. Because he was closing in on his goal, he told himself. Though he would rarely indulge himself like this in the future, he would do so enough to ensure that she was his forever.

Catarina stirred. She opened her eyes and looked at him, the wonder in them still laced with pleasure. Her hair was mussed, her lips swollen. An echo of the word *mine* reverberated through him.

She smiled at him, and the smile was not a mask for polite company. This one was full of intimate pleasure. Before he could stop the thought, a future played out in front of him, a possibility of having something far more than he had ever imagined. It was a future where she smiled at him like this across the breakfast table, even when there was no paparazzi there to watch. It was a dangerous thought, so he pushed it away.

"I hope you are feeling all right," he said gruffly.

"Much better than all right." Her voice sang with humor and a touch of wonder that swelled inside him.

He should move. He should take care of her somehow. He was not in the habit of deflowering virgins and, frankly, knew little about what she might want next. Gently, reluctantly, he slid out from her, and it was then that he felt something was wrong. He froze as an icy chill ran through his veins. The condom had broken. He had spilled his seed inside her.

He stared down at the condom, then looked up at Catarina. The smile on her face faded into confusion, her eyes searching his. Then she looked down, too.

"Oh." It was just one word, so soft he almost didn't hear it. But he could feel the shift in her, and this shift sent another cold shock wave through his veins.

"We must get married immediately," he bit out instinctively. Even as the words came out of his mouth, he knew they weren't the right ones, and yet he couldn't stop them because all he could think was *scandal*. Her father had alluded to this kind of scandal on the first day when discussing a well-timed wedding, but that concern paled in comparison to the threat that filled him. The Carandini family could not have a child born out of wedlock. It was one thing for him to weather a scandal alone but quite another for him to subject the next generation to one before the child was even born. He would never allow that. Never.

But children were supposed to be an issue they'd

sort out far in the future, long after this electric connection had died out. Not now, when everything inside him felt so...volatile.

By the time Catarina's gaze met his again, there was an unreadable mask across her face, and a cold politeness rang in her lovely voice. It did something strange to him when she spoke. "We absolutely do not have to marry."

"I will not allow my child to grow up under scandalous conditions," he snapped, louder than he meant to.

"We don't even know if I'm pregnant." There was an incredulity in her voice that almost covered the shakiness. Almost.

A feeling was rising in him, a souring brew of all the emotions that the past hour had stirred in him. This recent turn of events bound them together in the most disturbing way. Massimo rolled off the bed and reached for the clothes he had tossed aside. His thoughts were too... tumultuous to continue this conversation, too chaotic to even hear one more word of protest out of her mouth, so he headed for the door. When he reached it, he turned around. Catarina hadn't moved. She was on her side, her hair cascading over her shoulder, half covering the breasts he still longed to take in his mouth. Still, despite everything. She wasn't looking at him. She was staring out the window with an expression that looked too much like resolve for him to contemplate further.

"We will get married," he said, his voice steady despite the tremor that resonated deep inside. "I will do everything in my power to make sure of it."

CHAPTER NINE

CATARINA WAS AS still as death as Massimo's footsteps disappeared down the hallway. She didn't move as she heard the creak of his door. But when the door slammed shut, she rolled onto her back on the bed, a place that was supposed to be her own. This room had always been a refuge, but as she took a deep breath, his intoxicating scent still lingered everywhere. Catarina wanted to scream. She wanted to cry. Most of all, she wanted to run far away from this man who made her weak.

I'll take care of you. Massimo's words had taunted her with a promise she so dearly wanted, and now they haunted her. It had taken her a moment before she realized that he was simply referring to sex, nothing more. He seemed completely unaware that they were the words that her father had used in their marriage discussion. He was simply clarifying that he would make sure this first time would hurt as little as possible, and he had shown her a tenderness that had evoked that stubborn hope that she couldn't seem to shake, the hope for *more*.

Catarina balled her fists in frustration. Even if his promise had only been for this one act of intimacy, it was still a lie because right now, everything hurt worse than she ever dreamed it could. Worse than it should have. Massimo had shown an unexpected passion, and somehow it made this ending even more heartbreaking. She had been so very right to be wary of his autocratic statements because the moment the evening took an unexpected turn, the tenderness disappeared, and the cold demands returned.

But his demands weren't the most disturbing part of the awful ending of their encounter. The hardest part to digest was the fact that, as he walked away, she'd had to bite her lip to stop herself from calling out to him, begging him to come back. Her body craved his. She craved his touch, his warm, hard chest against her, his big hands splayed across her back, holding her close, and the long, hard length of him deep inside her. She *needed* him again. There must be something wrong with her, she decided, to want someone who had completely and treacherously turned on her.

Because the last thing she wanted was to start a family with a man who clearly could not—no, would not—love her. Who would not give her the respect she deserved.

Catarina blinked up at the ceiling as outrage competed with the intoxicating memory of his mouth everywhere. She needed to sleep. Everything would look better in the morning. She pried herself out of bed to wash the tears from her face, then returned to bed, burying herself under the covers until somehow she fell asleep.

Her sleep was fitful, her dreams, vivid, erotic and

haunting, but when she awoke in the morning, the music returned. It was playing through her head with the clear ring that she used to awaken to every day. But the tune that played was one that had captured her imagination in her teens and then haunted her dreams in the days after her mother's passing, Rachmaninoff's Prelude in C-sharp Minor. Now it called to her with an intensity she could not ignore.

Yesterday she had sat on the piano bench, the familiar cool wood under her welcoming her back as the music filled her, but she had not been ready to let it out, to reveal the emotions that brimmed inside her. Today was different. Today they would not be contained. They seeped through her defenses, through her carefully constructed facade and made her vulnerable.

And in the same way Massimo's kiss had taken over yesterday, consuming her, she felt consumed by the need to play. Something deep inside ached, something that, if she was honest, had ached for years, begging to be free. She had been an obedient daughter and ignored this wild intensity inside, but last night something had shifted. She might carry a child of her own. She could no longer sail through her life, allowing the winds around her to guide her course. Catarina owed this child her protection, the protection her father had not given her, despite his good intentions.

Catarina didn't bother to dress or wash her face or do any of the things that she was taught to do to make herself presentable. She simply rose from her bed, brushed her hair from her eyes and descended the stairs, her gaze fixed on the piano.

Outside the window, the wind had let up, and the fjord was just visible through the fat flakes of snow that fell like feathers, drifting back and forth in the gray morning. A soft, diffuse light lit the piano as she approached it, as if it were calling to her.

Catarina opened the bench and rustled through the music until she found the right piece. Her heart pounded as she propped it on the music stand, took a deep breath and played the first notes of the Prelude that had haunted her. The music seemed to swell inside her. She began with the heavy chords, feeling the foreboding that echoed in each one. When the chords changed into arpeggios, picking up speed and turmoil, all in that haunting minor key, she was swept away into the turbulent progressions up and down the keyboard until they came to the end in a clatter of chords. She entered the final lines, heavy and absolute. Breathless, her hands hovered over the keyboard. She expected to find herself crying. That had been her worry the previous morning, that her music and her sorrow were inextricably intertwined. But what she felt was more complicated than sorrow.

The room came back into focus, and Catarina was suddenly aware that she was not alone. She looked over her shoulder and saw Massimo, standing at the base of the staircase, his expression inscrutable.

Awareness shuddered through her, that now-familiar lick of hot desire, along with the protective urge to suppress all signs of it. The best course of action was to put all of these thoughts aside and examine them later when they had returned to Milan and she was in the safety of her room. She could sort them out the way she always had, alone. But even the thought of returning to her father's house, back to safety, was no relief.

She attempted to school her features, to push down her feelings the way she had spent years practicing, but Catarina found that she…couldn't. Something had broken free inside her, something she could no longer suppress.

"What were you playing?" he asked, his voice so much gentler than she'd expected.

"Rachmaninoff's Prelude in C-sharp Minor," she said, and she could hear that her voice was still tinged with the dizzying turmoil of the music that had started to untangle the mess of emotions knotted inside her. "It is said that the composer wrote it after a dream of his own death."

"That was…stunning," he said, and his eyes now seemed to be filled with open admiration.

Her breath caught in her throat as the knot tightened inside her once again. Would he simply talk to her like this, as if nothing had happened? Yesterday he had dangled a different kind of future in front of her, a future that included long evenings of food and conversation and unspeakable passion, and then, when the condom broke, he had so viciously yanked it away. And now he was complimenting her on something she held so dear. What was she supposed to do with this man?

"The piano holds no judgment of me for the times my thoughts are less palatable to those around me," she replied, and her voice wavered with emotion. Why couldn't she say this in the careful tone she had practiced her whole life? How could she have let herself get this out of control, exposing herself, making herself so vulnerable in a way that she could no longer take back?

She had meant her comment as a subtle reference to her less than generous feelings toward him, but if he understood this, he didn't take offense. In fact, in his gaze she found something that looked like understanding. Real understanding. Maybe he was looking for a way forward, a way to talk through the possible consequences of the broken condom. The flicker of hope wasn't nearly as strong inside, but it was still alive.

The room was quiet, and he said nothing, just gazed at her. And in that moment, a roller coaster of emotions raced through her, one that seemed to mirror what she saw in Massimo's dark eyes. She saw hope. Fear. Joy. Frustration. And with every peak and valley was that insistent desire that never seemed to go away with Massimo. The air seemed to charge between them, but before she could think through this, he looked away.

"The storm seems to have abated," he said, gesturing out the window. "I imagine I will be able to contact my helicopter soon, and we will return to Milan. I expect that things will be clearer then."

She could hear the implication behind these words, that the moment she faced her father and the trappings of their lives again, she would soon bend to his will. Frustration took over, and Catarina looked away, trying to hide any traces of the sinking feeling that she had been mistaken. Even misled. This conversation, this connection, was simply a lead-up to the next step in his plan. And her job was to fall in line.

"I find that things look perfectly clear from here," she said tartly as she tried to shut off every other complicated feeling that had been building inside her.

Both of them knew how much easier it would be if she simply gave in. This was why she had fled to her house on the edge of the vast fjord, wasn't it? Because being in Milan in her father's house, she felt the weight of her obligations to her parents and their vision of what her life should be.

Then Massimo had followed her here, and her private hideaway no longer eased this problem. Or maybe the safety of her mother's mountain home had only been an illusion. The struggle lived inside her as it always had, but Massimo had triggered these long-simmering emotions to erupt, and the problem cut deeper than the expectations laid on her. *She had chosen* to shape her life around these obligations. It was time for that to end. She took a deep breath. "I will return with you to Milan when the storm clears, but I will not marry you simply because there's a chance I am pregnant."

The unreadable expression on his face turned glacial. "Everyone has things that they need, Catarina," he said, his voice a low, unmistakable warning. "Some of us want to preserve our family name and others want to please our fathers, for example. These can be powerful motivators, and I find that people go to great lengths to ensure those needs are met. These most basic drives are impossible to ignore."

"Of course, you are speaking from experience," she said.

"I am."

Catarina found her temper flaring higher at the cold control in his voice, while her own wavered with emotion. Was he truly the same man who had lit up with passion, who had called out her name and looked at her like nothing in this world would pull him away? Yesterday must have been a lie, all of it. He had toyed with her emotions and satisfied his own desire. The only piece that she had to hold on to, the only thing undeniably real, was that desire. Catarina clung to the naked want she had seen as he moved over her, driving them both crazy with pleasure. If he was using his desire so recklessly, then she would use it, too.

Catarina stood and took a step toward him. Another. She caught a flicker of surprise in his eyes before the hardness returned, so she continued. He retreated, the wall now at his back, as his gaze traveled down her body. Awareness tingled in her breasts and between her legs. Just the brush of his gaze was enough to harden her sensitive nipples, and she felt the sensual scrape of her silk pajamas against them. His gaze momentarily fixed on her breasts, and she caught a flash of the heat that she had seen the day before.

Yes, this was the road forward. This was the only way she knew how to get through to him. She had tried to use her voice, and he was shutting her out, but she could use this, show him that he could not freeze her out, that he would not control her. Catarina took another step and another until she was almost flush with him. Her body exploded with heat, and her breaths were coming one on top of the other. There was no mistaking her intent, but he did not move.

He had schooled his face back to that impenetrable mask, and yet passion flared in his eyes. Massimo had started this battle of wits, and he was waiting for her to back down. She would not. He had done this to her, made her vulnerable, opened this Pandora's Box of her emotions. He had set them free, and now he would see the results.

"If things are as you say," she whispered, letting him hear her desire. "If I will, indeed, give in and marry you on your terms once my father is at the negotiating table, then I see no reason to hold back right now."

She lifted her hands to his cheeks. He had showered but not shaved, and the rough stubble contrasted with the soft fullness of his lips. She knew that she would lose herself soon again. That was inevitable. If he had entered her room this morning, she wouldn't have turned him away. She desperately ached for this man, and he had given signs that he might ache for her just as desperately. At least this could be a place where they met on equal ground, she told herself as she urged his face closer to hers.

He gave no resistance. His gaze did not lose its hard edges, but he didn't pull away. Her breath caught in her throat, and her heart took off in soaring arpeggios, higher and higher. The ache between her legs throbbed insistently, and no amount of logical thinking could make it stop. Instead, it grew and grew into something too strong to control. So when his mouth neared hers, she parted her lips, welcoming him. And when his lips descended on hers, she lost her mind.

* * *

This kiss was a trap. Something had shifted in her. Her expression was different, new. Back in his room just moments ago, his temper had been fully reined in, and his purpose, clear and unshakable. Massimo would pursue the marriage he had bargained for with the same relentlessness as he had pursued everything else in his life.

Then he had heard the music, and he'd found himself opening the door, moving closer. Catarina was playing the piano, and the slow succession of minor chords was so haunting that it took his breath away. It was as if his inner torment had been embodied in a piece of music. He only had a passing interest in piano, but he knew enough to hear that this feeling was about more than simply the notes. It was just as much about the skill and passion of the musician who was bringing the piece to life.

Massimo's thoughts jumped back to the image of Catarina the previous morning on the piano bench, sitting still, her face marked with traces of passion, and maybe even ecstasy. Something had twisted in his gut, something that he did not want to acknowledge.

And then the music was over. Massimo was conscious that he had descended the stairs, moving closer as she played. He'd tried to summon the righteous indignation that he had felt since he had left her room the night before, as he had built the story in his head, turning Catarina into his mother, but it didn't come. He was struck with the uncomfortable knowledge that, with his anger stripped from him, a powerful want took over, relentless.

When Catarina finally turned to him, her hair was a wild tousle of waves, and her eyes flickered with unfiltered passion that he had seen as she fell apart in his arms the night before. He could sense the power inside her, growing and transforming. She was blooming, and he couldn't bring himself to dislike it, even though she was turning this newfound power on him. Massimo was caught between the dual instincts to watch her break free of the cage that she kept herself in but also to pull her in so tightly that she would never escape. She was dangerously enchanting.

As she urged her lips closer, he reasoned that he could not turn away from this passion now unleashed inside her. If he resisted, would she turn this passion elsewhere when they returned to Milan? The question rattled him to the core, shaking every piece of the stony hardness that he had used to brace himself. As he felt the last of his resistance crumble, he could not bring himself to care, not when her lips were on his. He would make her his.

Satisfaction surged inside him as she seemed to soften to him. He no longer had to resist the maddening pull between them that had kept him awake all night. He brought his lips to her mouth, and the relief of touching her again was usurped by something far less tamed. She responded immediately, opening for him, kissing him with wild abandon. Her hands tangled in his hair as she drew him closer, taking from him greedily, stoking this fire that burned so brightly between them. Her lips were velvety soft as she kissed him with a desperation that spiraled so quickly out of control. He pulled her against him, his hard length meeting her softness. The moment their bodies connected, he left behind the notion of control and negotiation.

"I don't have another condom," he bit out roughly.

"That's okay," she said.

Massimo shuddered with a surge of possession that overtook all other thoughts. Last time the broken condom had been a mistake, but right now, he was suddenly gripped with the thought that he could throw all this uncertainty away and make her his. This time for sure. And though the idea of a baby rattled him to his core, he suddenly wanted this irrevocable bond between them more than he feared the consequences. It defied every last rational thought.

But then she was lowering herself to her knees, and he realized that she had an entirely different idea in mind. Not sex without a condom. Not giving in to the voice that thundered *mine* inside him. But before his mind could fully register his own shocking reaction, she had made quick work of his belt and pants, and now her slim fingers fumbled with the last layer between his length and her mouth. If he were a better man, maybe he would have resisted the mix of lust and innocence in her eyes. It made him wonder if he would survive this with his sanity intact, but he didn't stop her.

Catarina took him out. She looked up at him through dark lashes, then back at his thick length. *Dio*, this was too much for any man to resist. Her lips parted, and she tasted him. Pleasure rippled through his body, but he gritted his teeth, letting her explore. Then, finally, she took him into her mouth. He let out a deep groan. Her hands searched, inexperienced, and he moved them, showing her how to hold him, guiding her fingers to the places that brought him most pleasure. She eagerly followed his lead, then continued with new explorations that were all her own, leaving him shuddering on the brink of bliss. She took him deeper, deeper, as he slowly lost his mind. His hands came to her hair, and she eagerly pleasured him until he couldn't hold back. The ecstasy came on so quickly he almost missed warning her, but when he bit it out, she didn't back away. She took him in one more deep stroke, and he released, calling her name.

Massimo collapsed against the wall as aftershocks racked his body. In his haze of bliss, she stroked him gently, then straightened his clothes, caring for him with a tenderness that was heartbreaking. Then he found himself on his knees, too, easing her onto her back on the soft rug at the base of the steps. He moved her silken panties off her lovely hips, moved between her knees and worshipped her. He worshipped her until she was panting, then moaning, then finally calling out his name. She moved and shook and came, and he drew out every ounce of pleasure with the slow caresses of his mouth. He felt a surge of satisfaction in her pleasure. Time had stopped. Nothing mattered except this moment.

She blinked once, twice, as if falling back into reality, then lifted herself to her elbows and looked at him. Her eyes were unfocused, half-lidded with drunken pleasure. The thrum of the word *mine* pulsed through him, threatening to overtake everything else. He wanted to carry her to the bedroom and discover all the uncharted pleasure he was only beginning to imagine between them. He needed to share a bed with this woman every single night. And then another image came to him, unbidden: This was the woman whose belly could grow round with a baby. His baby. The unsettling idea hit him, shaking him with the feeling that he refused to identify this time. Still, he couldn't now unthink the picture in his mind of Catarina pregnant, nor could he forget the word that continued through the murky cloud of his thoughts: *mine*.

He shoved this word deep down inside as he gathered the last threads of his self-control.

"We will marry," he said, and he was relieved to hear the hard, implacable edge to his voice.

She rolled her eyes. "It's kind of cute you still think this method of persuasion will work on me."

The sarcasm in her voice was cutting.

"We have to," he insisted, but it came out more like a plea.

"Why?" Her voice was softer now. "You have heard me say I don't want this path. Why do you keep insisting?"

Massimo swiped a hand over his face, trying to control this rush of emotions that threatened to destabilize him. How did he explain the harm his parents' lives had infused in every part of his for far too long? He didn't have the strength for that, not now. So he fought for control over the hurt and need and leveled her with his gaze. "Be ready to leave when the helicopter lands."

* * *

Catarina sat on the soft red rug in the great room, her body alive with the pleasure that still pulsed through her. He had given in to the temptation of her kiss quickly and eagerly, and so had she. Tasting his hard length, so erotically tempting, and the intense satisfaction in Massimo's gaze as he'd pleasured her, had tipped her over the edge into bliss. The heat between them was undeniable, but she was no longer sure if she had wielded it or if this electric connection had taken on a life of its own. After playing the scene over a few times in her head, she found herself thinking about the moment when she had answered Massimo's comment about the condom. The look on his face had been so strange and wondrous, and she might have written it off as excitement about the prospect of the pleasure she was offering, except that it changed when she got to her knees. He looked almost…disappointed? In that moment, she had had the strangest feeling that he had *wanted* sex without condoms. That he had wanted the possibility of a baby.

This defied all her assumptions. Up until that moment, she had assumed that he saw the possibility of a baby as an unfortunate outcome of their actions, an assumption backed by the evidence of his cold declarations about illegitimate children and the duty to his family name. But the glow in his eyes made her wonder if she had missed something important.

Slowly, she got to her feet. Her knees were still weak. Her whole body was weak. But as she started up the steps, Massimo appeared on the landing. He was fully dressed, as if he had just emerged from a business meeting and not from the abyss of sex. His chiseled jaw and sharp cheekbones looked even more sculpted in the morning light. He looked like the man she had seen in her father's library, a hard, exacting man who used his authority ruthlessly, so far from the man who had looked at her with overwhelming hunger. And yet, his full lips taunted her, reminders of the pleasure they could bring. Catarina crossed her arms, unwilling to expose the path of her thoughts, but Massimo's gaze had already drifted down to her breasts, and there was a sudden burst of lust in his eyes before the ice-cold veneer sharpened again across his face.

"The phone service is back, and I have called a helicopter to fetch us," he said in a voice that was hard and final. "It will arrive in fifteen minutes."

He didn't wait for her answer. He turned and disappeared into his room. Catarina stared at his door, trying to process this new piece of information. They were no longer snowbound. She should be relieved. She *was* relieved. But her treacherous body protested, suddenly not ready for it to end. Not like this.

Massimo hadn't bothered to ask if she planned to leave with him. Of course, this made her want to insist that she would not, to put her foot down with this autocratic man. Her next instinct was to flee, but Catarina had already learned that he was a force she could not outrun. Not when the pull to stay near him came from inside herself.

Should she protest? Insist that she stayed here? Certainly, he would not carry her out to the helicopter against her will…would he? A part of her wanted to test him, just to see how far he would go to bend her to his will. Or maybe she already knew the answer. That was what disturbed her. But staying meant waiting for the avalanche dig-out, then the plow, then a tow truck to take his car, which was still buried in the snowbank at the end of her driveway. And after that, she'd need to summon the family jet, which her father had certainly called back to Milan. All of that would take time, and she wasn't sure she wanted to be alone in this house when she discovered whether she was pregnant.

Pregnant. The idea rattled around in her, almost too big to contemplate. She craved the closeness she had felt with her own mother. What would this relationship feel like from the other side? It was a responsibility she wasn't sure she was ready for. But if a baby was already on the way, she had to be.

She showered and gathered her belongings, and fifteen minutes later, Catarina found herself walking through the deep snow, toward the landing spot Massimo had managed to scope out. She was thankful for the loud thump of the propeller, then for the driver listening through the headphones because it meant that she didn't have to speak to Massimo beyond a bare minimum on their way down the mountain.

On arrival at the airport, she managed to summon a few polite words of thanks for the pilot, ingrained into her as deeply as anything else. As she walked up the steps to his jet, she reminded herself that in a few hours, she would be free to sort through these strange emotions stirring inside her. She would be free to fall apart again if she needed to. But for now, she just needed to get through this flight back to Milan.

Catarina settled in a plush leather armchair and turned to face the window. Massimo could have chosen any other seat on the jet, but he chose the one across from her, so that if she looked forward, she would get the full effect of his demanding gaze. Even out of the corner of her eye, she was aware of the strong jawline she had traced the night before, the broad, muscular shoulders that had held his powerful body above hers as he sank deep inside her. Her cheeks heated. Just Massimo's nearness usurped the carefully cultivated persona she had always presented to the world. Catarina reminded herself that she was above anything as petty as telling him to find a new seat or moving herself, so she focused studiously on the sparkling blue sea that spread out underneath them as the plane climbed into the air.

"I will arrange for a marriage within the week at the church," said Massimo as they leveled to cruising altitude. "I understand that you want an extravagant celebration, but we must ensure that the timing leaves no doubt about the legitimacy of this child."

"You have no idea what I want," she snapped.

Massimo raised his eyebrows, and his eyes flashed with heat. "Are you sure about that?"

His tone was unmistakably carnal, and her body simmered with the truth of these words. She swallowed and looked out the window, trying desperately to escape his gaze, to rein in the heat and temper that pulsed inside her.

"*If* there is a baby," she started, putting the emphasis

on *if* and ignoring the feeling that the word *baby* created within her, strange and unexpected, "this child will be loved and cared for regardless of our marriage status. That holds far more importance in my mind than your worries about what you call legitimacy. No child of mine would ever be made to feel illegitimate, whatever decisions *both* their parents decide to make."

Catarina slowed on the word *both*, and she said it in the measured voice that she endlessly practiced over the years, all without taking her eyes from the vast blue of the sea passing below them.

Even without looking, she sensed Massimo did not react well to this answer. When he finally spoke, his voice held a chill that made her shiver. "A Carandini heir will not be born under threat of scandal. We *will* marry."

She turned to him and narrowed her eyes. "You might want to think back to what happened the last time when you demanded the terms of what I will or will not do."

He looked away, and the lips that had been so soft against hers now formed a hard, thin line. Catarina flashed back to the look in his eyes the last time he demanded marriage. It was almost...bleak. *He was in pain.* Her reaction was visceral, the memory twisting in her gut. Something about their relationship scraped at his wounds, wounds that seemed to be somehow caught up in the Carandini family name and history. This understanding settled inside her, shifting her frustration into something more complicated.

Catarina took a deep breath and tried again. "If you

want me to reconsider, you need to give me reasons. Why must we marry? Why is your family name so important to you? Talk to me. *Please*."

Massimo flinched at this last plea, but he said nothing. She returned her gaze to the jagged coastline that marked the European mainland, but before she could fully look away, she caught a glimpse of an expression she had seen before, the one she could only call tumultuous. Was this the expression of a man determined to bend her to his will, even if it meant breaking her, or was this something more?

The cabin of the jet was silent. Massimo must have somehow indicated to the flight attendant not to disturb them because there was no sign of anyone else. There was only Massimo across from her, his imposing body too present to ignore. The longer she sat close to him like this, the longer she could feel her body softening, longing to touch him again. It was torturous to know that he was capable of such passion and tenderness, and yet also capable of cutting it all off so coldly and suddenly. All because the condom broke. All because of the threat of an unplanned pregnancy. All because he wanted an obedience she would not—could not—give him. Not without breaking.

She caught her first glimpse of the Mediterranean, sparkling in the distance out their window. The flight was almost over.

When Massimo finally spoke, his voice was grave enough to make her turn. "Do you know the story behind the bankruptcy of our family company?"

"Only vaguely."

"The company had been on a long descent since my grandfather's stroke forced him to step back from the day-to-day running of the business. But the turning point was on the eve of our parents' anniversary when they invited friends and business associates for a weekend on the 'company' yacht. They had anchored on a reef off a remote island and their day unfolded in its usual chaotic way. Just this close-up view of their relationship would have likely been enough to end some of these relationships." Massimo grimaced, and Catarina could see that recounting this story was causing him pain. "The night escalated to throwing glasses and plates and culminated with my father's demand to return to the mainland immediately. After a shouting match with the captain about protocols, my father got his way. It was only when they had returned to the wharf that some poor crewmember was allowed to point out that they had left two people behind—the president of a major shipping company they were in negotiations with and his wife. The crewmember remembered spotting the two alone in the dark waters, taking what they had intended to be a quick and romantic skinny dip. Later they learned the couple had been forced to swim over a kilometer to shore and, upon coming to land, had stumbled along the rocky beach, naked, until they had found a small fishing hut. They had spent the subsequent few days hospitalized with hypothermia."

"That's awful," she said, almost to herself.

"Even without that terrible end, business relations would have likely soured after that evening, though neither of them ever seemed to understand that. To this day they blame the crewmember for not speaking up sooner." Massimo's expression flashed with disgust. "The disaster on the yacht was just the exclamation mark at the end of a long and winding story of the downfall of my father's reputation and, thereby, the Carandini family's. The day the news reached my grandfather, he had a second stroke."

"Oh, my." Catarina wanted to reach for him, but he felt so very far away right now.

"Alessandro and I have dedicated our lives to rebuilding the company. We have sacrificed everything for it. And yet, we cannot shake the suspicions that we are one step away from self-destruction. Business partners, the paparazzi…" Pain slashed across Massimo's face again. "Alessandro is better at handling the pointed humor than I am. But it still haunts both of us every day of our lives."

"A baby out of wedlock would trigger more suspicions," she added, understanding falling into place. His expression softened as he met her gaze, and for a moment she felt their connection before he looked away. His actions over the past few days were finally starting to make sense. Massimo carried the burden of his family's past on his shoulders, and it was crushing him.

His gaze was solemn. "Maybe Alessandro, with his well-known flings, could get away with it, but not me."

"It must be hard to live like that. Always vigilant," she said softly. "Your parents must be grateful for everything you've done."

The corners of his mouth turned down.

"The most generous interpretation of my parents' relationship with my brother and me is that the intensity of their fights and passionate reconciliations doesn't leave them the energy to consider their impact on their children. The likely truth is that they simply don't care." He kept his eyes on the window, and his expression was stark.

"I'm so sorry," she said.

"I've had a lot of time to think about how two people could become so careless, and I still haven't come up with anything other than selfishness. I will do everything in my power to make sure no child of mine has that experience."

There was an anguish in his words, a despair that suggested his demands were about so much more than his getting his own way. He had alluded to his parents' absence over dinner as the background to the summer he and Alessandro spent at their grandparents' estate; but this time, she heard devastation in his voice. And why wouldn't it be there? He had been a boy once. Vulnerable. Catarina had lived her entire life around her mother, and this loss was still a gaping hole, even four years after the funeral. His parents were still alive yet forever out of reach.

Just a man.

"I'm so very sorry this was your experience," she said quietly. "But I'm sure you know marriage doesn't have to be like this."

"This is a risk." He gestured between the two of them as the dam of his emotion threatened to burst. "For the last two days I could think of nothing but you. And the idea of a baby…" He shook his head. "Everything could fall apart again."

Catarina thought back to those first moments in the library of her home. There had been a connection between them, and he had tried to quash it. *Just like he was doing right now.* She wanted to reach for him, to comfort him, and yet she was almost sure he would turn her away. Where did she go from here?

"I should know within a week whether or not I am pregnant," she said. "We can decide what to do from there."

He was silent.

"If there is a baby, another week won't matter," she added.

"We cannot ignore the engagement dinner I scheduled." Just a few days ago, she may have mistaken this stillness, this blank look, for detachment, but right now, she understood that there was a well of emotion behind it. But that didn't take away from the fact that he was still pushing the engagement, despite everything she had said.

"We can *discuss* it," she replied. "But first, I need a little space to think this through."

He must have heard the determination in her voice because he didn't push further.

Catarina had little memory of the landing or the silent car ride back to her home in Massimo's Ferrari. He didn't even look her way when she climbed out of the car, and she told herself that it didn't hurt, that this is what she had wanted. Space to think. She climbed the front steps of her family home and entered through the intricately carved doors. Gianluigi, their butler, greeted her with a deferential nod as she walked through a vast hall, with its high, vaulted ceilings and plaster flourishes, along the deep red carpet that trailed down the center. She passed one heavy wooden door, then another, pausing as she came to the doorway to her father's office, then continuing through the familiar halls until she came to her suite. She opened the door and found everything exactly as she'd left it. The delicate covers and pillows were neatly arranged on an antique bed, and her collection of childhood books sat on the corner shelf, next to her reading chair. It was all achingly familiar, and yet the room didn't bring her the relief she'd expected. It felt as if it belonged to a distant version of herself.

The past few days with Massimo, she had argued with him, slept with him, stood up to him and, most painful of all, fallen for him. But somehow, this journey had all become a discovery of herself, too. She couldn't stay here. In fact, she should have moved out long ago, she realized.

So she closed the door to her room and walked through the hallways, thinking of all the people in the world who lived in cages of one form or another, cages that were imposed on them by others. She was not one of those people. It occurred to her that, at this point in her life, the cage she was in was actually self-imposed. The risk of disappointing her father had coaxed her to avoid conversations with him about what truly would make her happy. She had made that decision herself out of fear, out of wanting to please and honor her parents. But as she walked through the hallways, she vowed not to stay in this cage of her own making any longer. Had it always been this easy to push open the door and fly?

Or had the hindrance been less about flying itself and more about what she wanted to do once she was free?

Catarina came to a stop in front of the door of her father's office again. This time, she knocked.

"Come in." Her father's voice was a familiar gruff bark, and when she opened the door, she found that he did not look the least bit surprised to see her.

"Massimo told me you would be arriving shortly," he said, treating her to a hint of a smile that so rarely came these past few years. "I hear wedding plans will be sooner than expected."

Massimo had clearly called her father, just another move to ensure she acted according to his will. Even after she had told him she was open for negotiations. Why did his betrayal surprise her? *Because you're still hoping for more from him.* But this betrayal cut too deep. He was pushing her too far.

"I have not agreed to the marriage yet, Papa," Catarina said, and her voice was stronger than she expected. "I want to move to the flat in Milan this afternoon."

Her father blinked at her, as if this was the last thing he had expected her to say. He opened his mouth to speak, then closed it, and she felt the bars of the gilded cage around her rattle. The sun hovered behind him, casting shadows on his face, and she noted the lines and wrinkles, the gray streaks in his hair that seemed to multiply daily. She used to see him as a man who outsized the world, but since her mother's death, he had grown smaller. He was growing older. She felt an intense love for him, a closeness despite the fact that he would probably never understand her.

"I know you want what's best for me," she continued. "It must have been hard to watch me struggle with Mama's death."

He turned away, as if even hearing these words was too much, but not before she saw hints of devastation he was trying to hide from her. Her mother's death had left her so afraid of the grief-shaped hole inside her that she had retreated from her own life. It was no wonder her father had grasped at something, anything, to try to help her.

"You are all I have left, my love," he said, and finally, he turned back to her. For the first time since her mother's funeral, she saw tears welling in his eyes. Her own lips trembled.

"I'm going to be all right. I will make sure of it." As she spoke these words, she could feel they were true. Even though everything hurt right now. Even though she had no idea what her future looked like, she would make sure she was all right. For the baby, if there was one, and for herself. "I need to do this on my own."

"Whatever you need, it is yours," he finally said. "I will alert the staff to your arrival."

As she walked out of his office, her hand came to her stomach. For the first time, she was on her own. Being alone had become her worst fear, and she had to face it before she made any more choices about her life. Especially since a pregnancy would mean she wouldn't be alone for much longer, no matter what happened with Massimo.

CHAPTER TEN

MASSIMO STARED AT the photo on page ten of this week's edition of *Gente* magazine. Someone had taken the picture on the tarmac of the airport where they'd landed, and it showed Massimo escorting Catarina into his Ferrari. He hadn't even thought to scan the area for paparazzi. He had been too focused on Catarina, and the look on his face in the photo was undeniable proof of the level of his distraction. It was obscene. Never had Massimo looked as much like his father usually did, fawning after his mother.

The conversation on that plane ride had dragged up emotions that should have stayed buried. And yet, he had found himself reopening old wounds for her, leaving him raw enough to let himself look at her like *that*. He needed to secure this marriage and then stay far away from Catarina. This was no longer simply strategy; it was the only way he could hold himself together. Clearly. And the baby? He had nine months to figure out how to handle that. For now, he needed to focus on the present.

For the past three days since their return, his assistant had combed the press, searching for any leaks of their broken engagement dinner. There had been mild speculations, of course, but this was different. This was much worse. The magazine arrived at the conclusion that there were clandestine motives at work, and he didn't bother reading further. To quiet whatever rumors circulated, he and Catarina needed to appear publicly as soon as possible. She had tentatively agreed to their engagement dinner, and following through on it would solve this current problem. Except Catarina had not responded to the seven messages he had left on her phone this morning.

Massimo tossed the magazine onto his desk and paced back and forth in his office. He glanced at the phone on his desk, tempted to call her once more. Instead, he stormed out the door and into Alessandro's office. He found his brother holding a different magazine, folded back to a page with the same photo. Massimo scowled.

Alessandro looked up from the magazine and studied him long enough to make Massimo squirm. He did not like to be studied, and certainly not by his brother, who seemed to be able to read his thoughts too well for comfort.

"She won't answer her phone," he thundered.

"You said she would contact you when she knew more." His brother's voice was maddeningly calm. "I agree your powers in this world are vast, but as far as I know they do not extend to speeding up the natural revelation of a pregnancy."

"Nor do I expect that," Massimo bit out. "But at least she could…"

His voice trailed off as he tried to capture the frustration that plagued him. Though Catarina had been correct in pointing out that waiting another week would not cause any more or less scandal, neither of them had foreseen this new development.

"It's quite a romantic candid shot of you," said Alessandro, his voice filled with irony. "You do, in fact, look…what's the word they used?" He glanced down at the magazine. "Ahh, here it is. Devoted."

Massimo could hear the censure in his brother's comments. The proposed marriage was supposed to quell speculations about the brothers' personal lives, not stoke them. Clandestine getaways with reclusive heiresses hardly presented a stable front. And if the paparazzi heard whispers of a pregnancy out of wedlock? They were doomed.

"Fix this, Massimo." His brother's voice was insistent. "There are other ways of getting in contact. You could go to her." Alessandro must have seen the way he stiffened because his brother added, "Or you could call her father."

Massimo had the urge to snap that of course he could do these things, but the truth was that he hadn't even considered them as real options. He hadn't considered much of anything that was rational, truth be told. So he gave his brother a grunt of acknowledgment that made his brother's lips quirk up into an ironic smile. But thankfully, Alessandro kept his mouth shut.

Massimo charged out of his brother's office and returned to his, slamming the door behind him. He came to a stop at a long window and looked out on the rooftops of Milan, the city spreading out in front of him. How could all his money and prestige and power count for nothing right now? What was the point of all this if he was still stuck here in agony? Because he ached for Catarina. He told himself he just wanted her in his bed, but even the thought of talking to her was enough to ease some of this relentless need. Just like his father. Massimo scowled, but he still picked up his phone.

Giuseppe d'Avalos answered on the first ring.

"Is Catarina at home?" Massimo's question was rough and abrupt, but it was the only way that he could stop himself from asking the question that pressed in his mind: Why hadn't Catarina returned his calls?

"She's gone."

"Gone?" Everything seemed to collapse inside him, and he didn't bother keeping the dread from his voice. "What do you mean?"

"She left for our flat in the city," d'Avalos said slowly. "I believe her words were something about dealing with this on her own."

Massimo heard the man's pointed emphasis on the words *on her own*, so he clung to the last thread of politeness and ended the call, then asked his assistant to find the address of the d'Avalos home in Milan.

Suspicions lurked in the back of his mind. Had she indeed left for their Milan flat, or was this story just a cover for yet another disappearance, this time more remote and difficult to track? The thought stirred a familiar frustration mixed with something far more dangerous, far more desperate.

Massimo left immediately, stalking through the

streets of Milan, trying to shake off some of the ominous thoughts that raced through his mind. He glared through the crowds of people on the sidewalk, all lost in their own worlds, so blissfully unaware of the torment that reverberated through him. His plans, his family's name, his sanity—Catarina was jeopardizing it all.

Massimo arrived in front of the tall building where she was supposedly staying, and the scent of roses blew by him in wisps, taunting him. The building was older and newly renovated, with gargoyles, stone flourishes and ostentatious columns as if to mark the legacy that the residents held in the city. He frowned as he walked through the marble corridor, muttering a few words about his fiancée to the doorman, who had his magazine open to the same article Alessandro had been reading. He looked at the photo of Massimo in the paper, then back up to the man in front of him. With a nod, he walked to the elevator and keyed it to the top floor.

The elevator groaned and creaked as it slowly made its way upward, trying his patience. The walk hadn't helped with his growing unease. Instead, a steely determination had grown as he'd stormed through the streets of Milan. He would demand that she answer his calls.

You might want to think back to what happened the last time when you demanded the terms of what I will or will not do.

Her words echoed inside him, laced with the soft temptation of her voice, and he felt the last shreds of his control fraying. He had spent his entire life making sure he would not be ruled by his emotions, and yet this appalling raw ache inside him was driving his every thought.

The elevator rattled to a stop and the doors slid open. Massimo barely registered the polished marble floors or the plaster flourishes that decorated the hall as he stalked to her door, raised his hand and knocked. He listened impatiently for her footsteps. Was she in the flat, as she'd said? Or had she fled yet again? Fleeing was exactly what his mother would do, he thought bitterly. How often had his mother left at a critical moment, giving only clues about her destination, expecting Massimo's father to chase her? He had to tame these brushfires of emotions and shake this feeling that was too much like despair. Because if Catarina had left, he knew he would scour the earth to find her. Which meant he was living out his worst nightmare. He was, indeed, his father's son.

Massimo was shaken out of these disturbing thoughts by the sound of soft steps behind the door, then the turn of the lock. The door opened, and she was in front of him, so breathtakingly beautiful his chest hurt. She was barefoot and wore a sundress in a pale shade of green that came down in a V, showing off her deliciously full breasts and cinching at her narrow waist. Her dark hair fell around her shoulders, and there were no traces of makeup on her lovely face. Catarina did not look like the proper society woman he had contracted to marry. Instead, she was a version of the woman he had seen in the Norwegian house, the one who wasn't keeping herself under careful control. He wanted *this* woman, he realized. He stared at the creamy skin that her dress revealed, thinking of the opportunities he had missed to taste every inch of it. Before he called the helicopter, he should have taken her to his room and let the fire between them burn one more time. He had squandered his chance.

Now he could not touch her. From the beginning, her touch had caused earthquake after earthquake, each one rattling him to the core, shaking the foundations that he had built his life on. He had given in to the temptation when they were alone, telling himself it was part of a careful seduction strategy, but in his heart, he knew that was a lie. Massimo had given in because no one tasted like Catarina. And when she had touched him, even the possibility of a baby born out of wedlock had not mattered. In that moment, he had *wanted* for her to be pregnant with his baby, regardless of the fallout. Which was madness. The last thing he wanted was to bring a child into the world while the Carandini name still carried the stain of the past. Children were not supposed to factor into this marriage until far, far in the future. And yet, in that moment, he had wanted a baby with Catarina, deeply and irrationally. Which was why he needed to stay away from her. But the siren's song of her voice and her body and every other element of her was irresistible, so the only option left was to tie himself to the mast of this marriage plan as they moved forward.

Catarina's eyes were wide, and she looked a little startled to see him. A burst of unwanted lust flared inside him, followed by frustration.

"Why did you ignore my calls?" he demanded.

The wonder dissolved from her face, and he silently cursed his heavy-handed outburst.

"Was I supposed to be available to you whenever you needed me?" she asked, and her achingly beautiful voice was cloaked with icy politeness. "I apologize."

He scrubbed his hands over his face. Why was he so hotheaded with this woman? He had never once struggled to maintain control with anyone else. It defied reason. Belatedly, he was aware that they were having this exchange in the hallway. In his experience, curious eyes and listening ears were everywhere, so ready to feed the next slice of juicy gossip about the Carandini family to the paparazzi.

"I'd like to move this discussion inside," he said. "Please."

The word *please* was a concession, along with the fact that he had resisted his instinct to order her, to demand what he wanted, an instinct he was increasingly understanding as desperation. And maybe she understood this because her polite expression softened just a fraction. After another breath, she stepped aside and indicated for him to enter, then closed the door behind him.

The hallway was bright and unexpectedly modern for the era of the building, but there were traces of its original form in the patterns of the wood floor and the intricate plaster flourishes around the doorways. Massimo noted each of these details, trying to divert his attention from the way the soft material of her dress so perfectly highlighted the roundness of her full rear. He ached to close the distance between them, to hitch up her skirt, plant his hands on her hips and take her against this carefully arranged wall, full of priceless art. He ignored the inconvenient stir in his groin and followed her into the living room. Catarina took a seat in a white armchair by one of the large windows that overlooked the city. At the far end of the room, sunlight reflected off the deep ebony of her piano, with books of music propped, one on top of the other, in front of the open keyboard.

He turned to her and focused on the reason he had come. "I called your phone several times. You didn't answer."

She sighed. "My phone is in the kitchen, and the ringer is off. I needed some time to think."

Logically, he was aware that the harder he pushed Catarina, the more she seemed immune to his frustrations. Yet, it still was a struggle to soften his tone. "And did this thinking lead you to any conclusions?"

"No conclusions, but things are becoming clearer, as you promised," she said with a polite smile.

He recognized that smile from the first day they had met. Her words were perfectly agreeable, though he was sure her thoughts were very far from that. The idea that this woman held in her hands a decision that would affect his life, a decision that he had no control over, was too disturbing to contemplate. Massimo had built an entire life around never having to be at someone else's mercy. His life was his own to control, and yet this control had slipped from the moment Catarina had entered his life.

And if she was pregnant... That thought was a clap

of thunder that threatened to shatter his thin veneer of calm. But there was still a chance that she was not, he reminded himself. There was still a chance he could walk away from this whole mess. Find another bride who actually understood the *convenient* part of this arrangement. But just thinking about leaving Catarina for someone else made his stomach feel as if it were in freefall.

"I would like you to answer my calls," he said slowly, grasping at the last threads of his self-control.

"I'll take that under consideration," she said crisply. "Now, please tell me why you are here."

When Massimo handed her the latest edition of *Gente*, Catarina's first instinct was to laugh. The idea of this stoic man spending the morning leafing through a notorious gossip magazine was absurd. But as she focused in on the photo he pointed to, all the humor inside her shifted into shock. She stared at it, frozen in place. Catarina remembered the exact moment the picture was taken, and her face flushed at the thought that someone else was watching. Heat traveled through her body as she recalled the gentle pressure of his hand on her back, the tender caress of his touch when he had helped her into the car, so at odds with the cold distance in his voice. At the time, she had told herself that the gesture was nothing more than politeness.

Catarina had spent the past three days trying to be rational about what had happened between them during the snowstorm. Massimo wanted a convenient marriage to an obedient wife, and he had used the spark of attraction between them to get it. It was that simple. He was definitely attracted to her, but he had made it clear on the plane that he would never let himself become close to her, not after he had seen his parents destroyed by what they thought passed for love. She could understand his frustration, as she had, in fact, agreed to a marriage of convenience. But that was before she had spent days with Massimo. Talked with him. Done those unspeakably hot things with him in bed. On the floor. And then learned what it felt like when he turned to ice afterward. She could no longer accept a distant marriage. It would be a prison, and he was determined to be her warden.

Yet, the picture in the paper gave her evidence to the contrary, evidence she could not look away from. The photographer had zoomed in, likely to validate their identities. But he had caught more than that. Catarina's own face was turned, focused on the step into the passenger seat of the Ferrari, but the shot showed Massimo's clearly, and it was full of raw emotion. He was looking down at her as if he was in love with her, despite his efforts to fight it.

Shock and confusion rattled her. She had spent the past three days trying to accept the fact that he desired her but did not—and would not—ultimately care for her. If she was pregnant, she needed their relationship to be on stable ground, which would mean putting her own feelings aside and making good decisions that kept their baby's best interests at the center of everything. She told herself that, under the right conditions, an accidental pregnancy wasn't the worst twist of fate. After all, she herself had been an unexpected baby, and her parents had never once made her feel like the pregnancy was a mistake. As long as their baby grew up surrounded by love, regardless of the parents' relationship.

Their baby. The words had played in her head over and over, threatening to overwhelm rational thought. Unlike Massimo, who had been brought up in a household where wealth was a substitute for parental attention, she had been surrounded with love, imperfect but wholehearted. Her parents had given her this, and she would give it to her baby. But the family she wanted right now was about more than children. She wanted a family with Massimo, this impossible, imperfect man who was capable of so much passion. He had shown her glimpses of tenderness, of the kind of connection she craved, and she wanted more.

Yet, his words on his jet had shaken her to the core. He seemed to believe that wholehearted love meant a self-centered destruction of everyone in his orbit. When she had arrived at the flat, she had spent the day scouring the internet for articles about his parents. As she read story after story in black-and-white, she could see that Massimo had, in fact, downplayed the dramatic public fights and equally public make-up scenes that his parents endlessly played out. What she hadn't fully calculated was how young Massimo was when this had all started.

Catarina understood where Massimo's conclusions about love came from. Maybe she would believe the same in his shoes. But that didn't change the problem at the heart of their relationship. Was she trying to fit a square peg into the nice, round fairy-tale ending that she wanted for their story? Maybe it was futile to convince him to embrace this passion between them. Maybe it was better to put her energies toward a compromise, so that by the time the baby came, the path was smooth. Over the past three days she had debated her choices, her heart and her mind at odds. Now, as she stared at this candid photo of him in the magazine, his expression so raw and open, it felt as if she were looking at a mirror of her soul.

She was falling in love with him. But if she said those words, it would only drive him further away from her. The thought was devastating. Catarina swallowed, then looked up at Massimo. As he gazed down at her, she searched for cracks in the facade of his hard expression. She found none.

"The photo is unfortunate," he said in that commanding voice he used with her, the one that frustrated her. But it also did strange things to her insides because she couldn't stop hearing the pain behind it, too. "We cannot wait a week for our dinner. To that end, I would *like* to make reservations for tonight."

At least he was attempting to ask and not simply commanding her presence. She tilted her head, studying him. "Surely, you don't imagine one public supper will smooth over all speculations. Won't it simply fuel more?"

There was pain in his reaction, a grimace, so small she might have missed it. But it was there. She took a step toward him. His eyes widened, and she felt a surge of satisfaction. This was what had cracked his hard exterior before. This was how they connected. And though touching him scrambled her own mind and softened her will, it was better than the cold reserve between them. Catarina lifted her hand to touch his face, but instead of giving in, he stepped back. His retreat felt like an arrow in her heart, but she told herself to ignore it. She told herself this was to be expected. Even if the photo told her Massimo felt the same as she did, he would resist it with all his being.

Catarina attempted to paste on a breezy smile. "I doubt this evening will be a PR success if you move away when I reach for you."

"There's no need to touch," he bit out, his voice rough and full of frustration.

She didn't back down.

"We are not your parents," she said softly.

His hard exterior seemed to crumble at her words.

"This—" He gestured to the remaining space between them. "This is madness. It can be twisted and manipulated and used for harm at any time."

Catarina's own frustrations took over then, laced with the heat and the heartache she was trying desperately to keep under control. "How can you say that? How can you ignore how good this feels?"

Massimo's eyes narrowed, and his expression was thunderous. "You're using sex to provoke me."

The accusation was a slap, and it traveled through her body, finding its way into her soul. It was useless to accuse him of the same because it only proved his point.

"I am trying to get through to you," she said, trying to keep her voice calm, even though her heart was breaking. Because she would absolutely not give him the dramatic meltdown he was expecting. "You shut me out the moment you sense a threat to you or your precious family name. You've built this—" she gestured at his tall, imposing figure, his hard expression "—this image of Massimo Carandini, made of impenetrable steel. You're not giving us a chance."

"This is who I am," he said in a voice that was hauntingly final.

"You are more," she whispered, but her words sounded like a plea.

He frowned and turned his back to her and started for the door. "I will pick you up at eight."

CHAPTER ELEVEN

CATARINA STEPPED OUT of Massimo's Ferrari, into the misty Milanese night. The evening rain had left a sheen that glistened on every surface. The city felt alive, washed clean and bubbling with car engines, laughter and the last of the rain spilling out of gutters, all mocking the tempest that had brewed inside her all day long. She wanted to show Massimo that they could be something different together, but the cold distance between them was too much to bear. The urge to turn away, to flee, to escape this pain, nagged at her.

The valet whisked the Ferrari away, and she was left standing next to Massimo. He wore a suit that emphasized his broad shoulders and narrow hips, and the collar of the crisp white shirt was unbuttoned, showing a glimpse of the dark hair on his chest she couldn't erase from her mind.

Sensations threatened to overwhelm her, the silk of her dress caressing her, and the cool night air on her bare legs. The warmth of her soft cashmere coat and scarf. The flare of desire that roared in Massimo's eyes when he opened her car door. All of these sensations contrasted with the hard, inscrutable expression he wore as they approached the restaurant. The well-dressed doorman opened the thick wooden doors, and she ached for the exquisite tenderness of his touch on her back, guiding her through the entryway and into the dark warmth of the restaurant. It never came.

Massimo said a few low words to the host, then gestured to the staircase that led to the second floor of the elegant restaurant, past curious onlookers. As he nodded to familiar faces, Catarina was reminded of just how much she disliked being in the spotlight. Her mother had always been the object of interest at high-profile appearances, drawing attention away from her, but here, she felt on display. She felt exposed right at the moment her defenses were down. But she had a plan, one that had kept her from listening to the old voice inside begging her to flee, run far away from the rawness she felt when she was near him.

Massimo led them to a circular table next to a window that curved out above the street. Though the distance from other guests gave them a bit of privacy, the table was visible to anyone who entered the second floor. Just the kind of audience Massimo had wanted, thought Catarina. It shouldn't bother her, this public theater of their relationship. After all, this was exactly what they'd planned, exactly what she had signed up for. And she did want to ease some of the gossip about their relationship that the photo had stirred up, at least to give them some space until they had an answer about the pregnancy. Still, it bothered her. Where was the man who had cooked for her and then worshipped her body with his? She wanted another glimpse of the man she had opened her heart to back in the remote cabin in Norway; the man who had shown her his pain on the plane ride home. Massimo seemed determined not to be that man.

He pulled out her chair from the table, making sure to keep his distance. The silver and glassware glistened under the light of the candles, and through the window the Duomo twinkled in the darkness. Just a week ago, she would have been perfectly satisfied with this evening, ready to play this role in exchange for the kind of freedom she had craved. Now everything had changed. Now that she knew what was possible between them, she could no longer settle for less.

The server came to present the evening's menu, and Catarina found her mind wandering to the impassive man across from her. She had absolutely no idea what he was thinking. When the server left the table, Catarina took a deep breath, then met his gaze.

"A few days ago, you asked me what I wanted," she said. "I have a new answer."

Her words had played through his mind all day, singing *You are more* in that silken caress of her voice, tempting him with a promise he knew wasn't real. The fire between them was a living thing, sparking to life at unpredictable times, taunting him to forget everything that he had spent his life building. Massimo should have felt suffocated by the oppressive heat of it. Instead, he burned hotter, the temptation growing stronger.

These dangerous feelings were starting to feel as inevitable as the tide, an unstoppable force of the ocean that flowed high on the banks of his self-restraint each time she was near. Now these vast, tumultuous waters were never out of sight.

A cloud of foreboding had hovered over them since he had picked up Catarina. He hated the calm facade she had masked herself with throughout the silent car ride. How maddening it was that he had sought her out for precisely this skill that was haunting him. Two competing desires warred in him: He craved the passion she had shown him every time they touched, and yet he absolutely could not tolerate the idea of a passion that threatened what was now and would always be his first priority, the redemption of his family's name. And even more maddening was the threat that lingered every time he considered this war of opposing forces inside him: He knew what happened when passion won this struggle. He had seen it play out for his entire life. And yet, he was still tempted.

But he would manage this point of vulnerability. He had successfully managed his parents until they were no longer a weakness but an obstacle he had overcome on his path to success, something to draw strength from. Though this success no longer felt like the balm it always had been. Still, Massimo had spent the evening telling himself that there was absolutely no reason to be uneasy. This supper was simply a formality, and yet he couldn't escape the feeling that something fundamental had changed since he had left her apartment earlier in the day. Now, as she sat across from him, her chin lifted in a hint of defiance and her lovely brown eyes clear, the foreboding cloud grew darker.

But Massimo Carandini had never backed away from a challenge. He and his brother had rebuilt an entire empire on their single-minded rebuke of their father's course in their quest to redeem their family's name.

He set aside these feelings, lifted an eyebrow and responded to her comment. "Just days ago, you said you had everything you needed. Has something changed?"

"Weren't you the one who questioned my desires?" she said mildly, though her eyes flashed with heat, as if she, too, was picturing the scene in the bedroom when he had held himself over her, taunting her with the question of what she wanted. Her heavy lashes fell for a moment, and when she looked at him again, the heat was gone. "I should think you would be happy to learn that I have reconsidered."

He dismissed the wisp of unease that ran through him, reminding himself that he was, in fact, happy that she had finally given in and come to the bargaining table. She would put forth her demands and he would reiterate his. Maybe the possibility of a baby was bringing out the practical side in her. *Their baby.* The words joined the unsettling mix of feelings that brewed inside him, but he kept them under control. "I eagerly await hearing of your desires."

Catarina straightened in her chair and leveled him with her gaze.

"I want a husband who loves and respects me," she said in a voice that was soft and yet devastatingly final. "Whether or not there is a baby..." Her voice wavered at this last word. "I want a family where love is at the center of all the choices we make together. Though I am far from ready for a baby, I will do everything to be the mother that our child needs, and I want the same from you. A child should be surrounded by love."

Her chest rose and fell, as if she was steeling herself for her next sentence. Massimo was frozen in place, unable to look away. It felt as if he was watching this slow-motion train wreck from the outside. For a moment, her gaze faltered. Her chest rose and fell again, as if she was shoring up strength. When she met his gaze again, her eyes were clear. "That is what I want from you, Massimo. Love."

A maelstrom of desperation and fury thundered through him. "And you are not willing to compromise on that at all?"

She shook her head, and he could see the determination in the set of her jaw and her unflinching gaze. This was not a negotiation at all. It was an ultimatum.

Massimo unclenched his teeth and kept his expression blank. "How can you speak of a life devoting yourself to the needs of your child when you are unwilling to compromise? I have already made far more concessions than I agreed to when I entered this bargain."

She swallowed, the movement in her long, slim neck betraying hesitancy.

"None of this has been what I agreed to," she said. "But I know now that there is no other way forward for me. Not with you."

He hated the waver in her voice, underlining the truth behind her words. And there was a part of him that needed to give her what she wanted. But she was asking for far too much.

It was as if she had pried open the most vulnerable part of him, exposing it for them both to view, right here in the restaurant. The bone-deep need to fight back against this feeling was overtaking him. He knew exactly what he needed to do right now. He needed to lie. He could promise her something vague, like that he would grow to love her. Just a few simple words that she needed to hear.

And yet...

He couldn't do it. Massimo stared across the table as the rush of emotions he had been fighting the entire evening hit him. He couldn't find enough air as he drank her in, paralyzed by her beauty, by the sound of her voice as it sang through him, by the overwhelming need to touch her again. He was paralyzed by *her*. She deserved what she wanted, and yet it would crush him if he gave it to her.

He swiped a hand over his face. "You are asking for the one thing you know I cannot give you."

Catarina did not try to hide the hurt that slashed across her face. "Then I suppose this conversation is over."

Massimo had little memory of what they ate or how they got through the excruciating meal. He no longer cared what observers at the tables around them detected, nor did he care about what might be written in next week's edition of *Gente*. The dignified lift of her chin was a devastatingly sharp knife that twisted each time he met her gaze, silently reminding him of what he knew he could not give.

The ride home was silent, and she didn't look at him

as they crossed the entry hall of her apartment building for the elevator. When the doors opened at the top floor, the only sound was the clack of their shoes on the polished marble floor. She stopped in front of her doorway, and he could hear her shallow breaths as she turned the key and opened it. The relentless charge between them sparked and surged, twinged with desperation. She was so temptingly close.

Catarina didn't step inside her flat. Instead, she turned and looked up at him, giving him another searching look. But this time, there was heat behind it, too. Massimo's body roared with the need he had contained all night. Frustration, desire and desperation conspired against him until he couldn't resist any longer. He leaned over and pressed his mouth against hers, tasting hints of wine and chocolate and, underneath, Catarina. Her hands came around his neck and slid into his hair. She was pulling him closer, kissing him the way she had kissed him in the snowbound house, with the passion and abandon that he couldn't get enough of. He kissed her like she was an oasis in the desert, one he couldn't bring himself to leave. She moved closer, pressing her body against his, and the need to take her right there, in the hallway, to make her his, to remind her of everything that he could give her, overtook him. *This is what you want*, said something deep inside him, ominous and clear. Massimo would never get enough of this woman. He would crave her for the rest of his life. Maybe this was his own twisted version of love, but he could not be a slave to it.

He clung to the last of his sanity as these instincts

threatened to overwhelm him. The desire to take her to her bed and spend the rest of the night making love to her would bring him to his knees. But he knelt for no one. It was a matter of survival. So Massimo Carandini used the last of his famous willpower, the strength that he had spent his entire adult life building, to pull away.

He looked into her eyes, half-lidded and hazy with desire. Her hair was mussed, and her lips were parted. He thrust his arms to his sides and clenched his fists, forcing himself not to reach for her again. Not to promise her everything she wanted just to spend the night in her bed.

"This hurts, Catarina," he bit out, his voice raw. "It's torturous. How can you want this?"

She lifted her chin, even as her eyes welled with tears. "I deserve love. I will not settle for anything less."

For once in his life, Massimo Carandini had no idea what to do next, so he did what his entire being was begging him not to do. He walked away.

Two days later, Massimo still had no idea what to do, which was how he found himself in his Ferrari, racing into the Italian Alps, ignoring the awful feeling in his stomach, as if he was in freefall.

He came to the familiar gates, then continued up the winding driveway, coming to a stop in front of his grandparents' towering country estate. Three rows of windows marked the floors of the main house, a symmetry interrupted by tangled vines of rambling roses that climbed the facade. As Massimo walked up the stone steps, he inhaled the familiar scent, then flashed to Catarina, to the same scent that lingered wherever she went. His mind finally made the connection it seemed to have resisted until now: Her scent reminded him of the only place that had ever felt like home.

Massimo looked up at the center window of the second floor, where his grandmother was almost certainly sitting in her reading room, awaiting his arrival. He climbed the remaining step and banged on the door with the brass knocker, a ghost of a smile playing on his lips as he took in its familiar lion's-head shape, knowing the housekeeper had likely been forewarned that his grandmother would answer the door herself. He waited, imagining her slow, regal steps down the grand staircase, her aging hands resting on the banister.

Finally, the door swung open.

"My boy," she said without a hint of irony, despite the fact that Massimo had so clearly left boyhood long, long ago. He bent over to kiss her soft, familiar cheeks.

Isabella Carandini had dressed for the occasion. Her hair was in a neat gray bun at the base of her neck. She wore a well-tailored dress in widow's black, a tradition she still held to after thirteen years. Around her neck was a simple strand of pearls with matching earrings that Massimo's grandfather had given her as a wedding gift, before he had made the kind of money that bought them family estates. During his lifetime, Massimo's grandfather had not been the easiest man, and yet Massimo never doubted the man's love for his wife.

"Constantina made her famous vanilla bean cake," she said, leading him through the long hallway, back to the solarium, where his grandmother spent her days tending to her plants. A table was set in the center of the bright room with her favorite porcelain set. There was a silver pot of coffee with creamer and the sugar bowl Massimo used to steal from as a child. The cake was dusted with powdered sugar, and on a silver tray at the side was a thin bottle of limoncello and two aperitif glasses.

He visited his grandmother less frequently than he should. When the thought crossed his mind, he told himself that it was his busy schedule, but there in her solarium, Massimo was reminded that his feelings about this house were complicated. This was the place where he had taken refuge when he was a vulnerable young teenager, and visiting it meant acknowledging a part of himself that he had left behind. Yet, he had cleared his schedule this afternoon to come. Massimo wasn't ready to contemplate what this meant.

His grandmother gestured for him to sit, and he inquired about her health and the health of her plants as he savored the slice of cake that she had neatly cut and served for him. When they had finished their coffee, she poured him a glass of limoncello and smiled indulgently as she handed it to him.

"I must admit your photo was the last thing I expected to see as I was reading my favorite gossip magazine this week." She lifted an eyebrow. "Maybe Alessandro's but not yours."

Massimo may have taken this as a provocation from anyone else, but there was sympathy and understanding in his grandmother's voice. She knew the depth of hurt that he had once felt from these kinds of headlines.

"Does your visit have something to do with the whispers I heard of an engagement?" she asked.

The words were perfectly polite, and yet he could still hear the rebuke behind them. He had planned to notify her of his engagement before his original supper plans, of course, but that was before the situation had careened out of control.

"I apologize for not calling you sooner," he said. "The situation has developed in unexpected ways."

She tilted her chin in acknowledgment, but he knew better than to mistake it for forgiveness. "Do you love this woman?"

Massimo grimaced. This should have been the easiest question to answer. Overwhelming passion, burning, aching need, possessiveness, even protectiveness—Catarina had wrenched each one of these feelings from him. But he was not capable of the kind of love she deserved. What he felt for her was already tearing him apart. Massimo had no idea what to call this pit in his stomach, this unwieldy heat, this voice that raged inside him, shaking him bone-deep with the word *mine*.

"I love her," he finally bit out. "And it will lead us both to our downfall."

"Don't be so dramatic, Massimo," she said with a wry laugh that pushed away some of the dark clouds that hovered over him. "Have you told this woman that you love her?"

"It's complicated," he muttered, looking away.

"I see," she said, and he had the distinct impression she did, in fact, see far more than he wished. She tilted her head a little, assessing him skeptically. "You must allow yourself happiness."

Massimo swallowed back a new and inexplicable twist of pain. Her words about happiness were so simple, and yet something inside him revolted against them. "And if I am not capable of this? If this feeling is devouring me from the inside?"

"Now you have convinced me that you are, in fact, in the throes of love." She gave him a smug smile.

"The kind of love my parents have?"

His grandmother's glass was halfway to her mouth, but she stopped. She set her limoncello back on the table and turned to him. All traces of her smile were gone.

"I know your father better than anyone in the world, and that includes your mother. He is my son…" She paused, and Massimo registered the grief in her voice. "And I can tell you that you are nothing like him. I should never have taken for granted that you understood that."

Her tone was breathtakingly serious. He stared at her as she lifted her glass and took a sip. When she looked at him again, there was a hint of challenge that sparkled in her eyes. "Anything you have learned about love from your father you can unlearn. You have defied his example in every other way. Why would love be any different?"

CHAPTER TWELVE

CATARINA STARED DOWN at the wand, lined up next to three others on a tray on her bathroom sink. Late at night, long after Massimo had left her aching in her lips, in her breasts and in her heart the previous night, she had awoken with cramps in her lower back. She had not allowed herself to analyze the sensation. Her body was speaking to her, but she was tired of listening to it.

Now the message was staring up at her, confirming her body's signals with a finality that she could no longer doubt. The tests were negative. She was not pregnant. Catarina sat down on the floor, allowing herself to fully register the familiar tenderness in her breasts, the familiar cramping. These sensations that she had experienced over the past few days, the ones that she had interpreted as signs of pregnancy, were simply the usual signals of the end of her cycle. Nothing life changing. There was no baby.

Catarina waited for relief to set in, but it didn't come. Instead, a strange stillness was settling inside her body, a numbness she was not prepared for. She had spent the past week worrying about the possibilities of a pregnancy she was far from prepared for, but with these possibilities came glimpses of a larger hope, not just for a baby but for something more, a hope for building the family that she craved. A family with Massimo.

Catarina took a final look at the row of pregnancy tests staring up at her, the single pink line unmistakably bright. Then she turned away and returned to the living room, sinking into her favorite armchair. On the table in front of her sat an enormous bouquet of red roses that had been delivered early in the morning. They seemed to sprout from the wide white vase, spilling over the edges with an excess that she couldn't stop staring at. The scent had filled her flat, intoxicating her, but the card was blank except for a large *M* scrawled across it. How fitting, she thought, to send something so intoxicating, excessive and yet withholding. Still, she ached for Massimo. Even when she should know better. She told herself the flowers were probably the work of his assistant, just another step in his well-calculated plan to make their marriage go through. And yet, her breath still caught when she looked at the bouquet. Her heart had swelled when her doorman delivered them. Wasn't this the kind of romantic flair she had wanted?

She reminded herself that Massimo had told her in no uncertain terms that he could not—or, rather, would not—love her. He refused to give her what she needed, and she knew that anything less would destroy her.

The threads that had held this marriage arrangement together had frayed. All she had to do to snap them was call Massimo and deliver the news that their pregnancy scare was over. And yet, she could not bring herself to do it. Not over the phone. But if she went to him, stood before him and once again welcomed that tempting pull that threatened to drag her under, would she be able to walk away? *Just a man*, she reminded herself. A man like the mountains that rose behind her house in the fjord, unmovable and impossible to ignore.

Catarina had no idea how long she sat in her living room, staring at the overflow of red roses, but finally, the swirl of anxiety and want that mixed with hope, that stubborn companion that dogged her, became too much. She left her apartment, not bothering to call her driver. Instead, she walked. Massimo's address was in a newer part of town, and the building was an impressive show of glass and steel. Catarina stopped outside the doors and stared up at it. It was infused with a starkness that she took as a reminder of everything Massimo Carandini was: powerful, impressive and remote. The truth of this visit hit her, paralyzing her in place: This was likely the last time she would see him.

"Catarina?"

His voice echoed through her, rich and deep, and the relief of hearing it was almost too much to bear. How was it that just his voice was enough to set off this electric current of desire that made her breasts heavy and her heart ache? She turned and found Massimo exiting his Ferrari, walking toward her with purpose in his eyes as the valet left with his car. As he came closer, the fire inside her jumped higher. His hair was combed back from his face, exposing the faint scar that healed on his forehead, and his eyes were dark and penetrating as he focused his gaze directly on her. She stepped back, trying not to be burned by it, but it was too late. It was as if something inside her was now linked to him, responsive to him in some deeper way. *It will always be like this*, said a voice inside her. This was a man who had made it clear that love was not on the table, who had stated he was done compromising. And somehow, this was the man she wanted. This was the man she had fallen in love with. It defied reason, and it was breaking her heart.

Catarina vaguely registered the people who passed them on the sidewalk, pausing to stare. A man in a three-piece suit holding a young girl's hand. A well-dressed woman with a fluffy white dog. Massimo must not have noticed them because she knew he would retreat from even this small hint of public display of emotion. His family's name and image would always come first. This last thought was the push she needed to speak.

"There is no baby," she said, keeping her voice low and clear.

His eyes widened, and Catarina wondered if he, too, had not fully considered their path forward without a baby to bind them together. The surprise in his expression was followed by a glimpse of something else, something that made her wonder if Massimo felt just as lost as she did.

"Please, let's talk about this in my flat," he said with a roughness that was heartbreaking.

Catarina shook her head. If they were alone, she wouldn't be able to resist him.

Massimo frowned down at her. "Perhaps we can move off the street? Just to the building's courtyard?"

Catarina swallowed. Anywhere public, he would never risk showy emotions, she reasoned. He would never reach for her or lean forward for one of his devastating kisses, the kind that seemed to stop time and erase all rational thought. So she nodded.

Massimo led her through the lobby, all glass and shining surfaces, but when he opened the door to the courtyard, her heart gave a painful squeeze. His building took up the entire block, and in the center of it was an oasis of green. It was as if they had been transported away from the noise of the street and into the walled grounds of a castle. There were plants everywhere, towering trees, fresh herbs and flowers on the ground and vines that clung to the fences and archways that separated the space into smaller, more intimate areas. It was as if she had traveled through his remote, carefully controlled layers and found the part of him she had longed for.

She knew she shouldn't hope, and yet she still did.

Restlessness had dogged Massimo the entire morning. After putting out a few fires, he had rushed to the jewelers' and paid the woman a diamond's worth to size the ring correctly while he waited. On the drive home, he played out potential scenarios, but when he stepped out of his car and found Catarina standing outside his apartment building, all his plans fell away. A powerful feeling shuddered through him, a surge of emotions too strong to ignore. His grandmother's words still echoed in his mind. *You must allow yourself happiness.* As he looked into the depths of her dark brown eyes, those words had stopped him in his tracks. His parents had caused so much pain in his life, and he was still letting their actions shape his. He had been on the brink of letting the fear of this pain take away his chance at love.

Now that Catarina was seated on the sofa of his courtyard, her shoulders straight, determined, he registered that this scenario was not one that he had considered. He had been prepared for arguments, contingency plans and reminders of everything at stake, but not the possibility that there was no baby.

Massimo was stunned by a bone-deep feeling of loss. At first, he thought it came from the loss of his plans, or maybe the idea of the baby, but as Catarina stared at him as if she was preparing to say goodbye, the truth hit him, a thunderclap that rattled his entire being. What if he was too late? He was losing *her*, and he absolutely could not let that happen. The desperation from this coming loss overwhelmed him, and in the chaos of his thoughts, one idea shone clearly: He could not lose Catarina out of the fear he had been running from his entire life, that in loving someone he would become like his father. The only clarity in front of him was that this fear was nothing in comparison to the devastation that would stay with him if she walked away. He could not let Catarina go.

"I was wrong about all of this," he started. Those simple words seemed to open a dam inside him, and all the feelings he had tried to repress tumbled through his mind. He loved her. Intensely. Desperately. But it wouldn't be his downfall; instead, it would be his salvation. As she looked up at him from the sofa, her eyes wary, he searched for a way to convey this seismic shift inside him.

Massimo slowly lowered himself to one knee. He pulled the jewelry box out of his suit coat pocket, then reached for her hand. Her breath hitched, and for one heart-stopping moment, he thought she'd pull away. But when her gaze met his, the wariness in her eyes was fading, and in its place, he found hope and a connection that reverberated inside him.

"I've fallen in love with you, Catarina," he started, not bothering to temper the raw emotion in his voice. "You deserve so much more than what I've offered you in these last days, but I will spend my life making it up to you. I want to surround you with the love you deserve if you will let me. Please, be my wife."

Catarina blinked at him, like she couldn't quite register what was happening.

"I thought you said you knelt for no one," she finally said.

"I kneel for *you*, Catarina," he rasped. "I kneel only for you."

These were words he never thought he would utter, and yet they felt like the truest thing he had ever said. Catarina's lips trembled as he opened the jewelry box. She looked at the ring, and then back at him. "You're carrying an engagement ring? In case the need arises?"

"My grandmother would be appalled at your reaction to this family heirloom," he said with a hint of humor.

Her eyes flared with longing, but she turned away. "You want someone who will play the role of a wife."

"I did say that," he admitted. "I've said a lot of stupid things."

"You did," she said evenly.

"Because I didn't allow myself to want more," he said softly. "I didn't think happiness was possible for me. Not with parents like mine."

He reached up and gently guided her chin so she was looking at him. She needed to see the truth he spoke. "I want you. I want to learn to be the husband you need. I want to love you the way you deserve."

Her gaze turned hot, and it blazed through him.

"You're all I think about," he continued, letting the thoughts he had so desperately tried to resist pour out of him. "I have spent the last week trying to find a way to deny this desperate ache for you, trying to tell myself that feelings this strong are toxic, but I'm done with that."

"This is going to hurt sometimes, Massimo," she said softly. "You said it yourself."

He ran his thumb over her lips, reminding himself that it wasn't too late to change. Not when he wanted to be with her like he wanted his next breath. "I'm going to need to learn to deal with the hurt. Someone much wiser than me pointed out that I have learned everything else out of sheer determination. Why would love be any different?"

"How sensible. Was this wiser person Alessandro?"

"*That's* your first guess?" He chuckled. "No. It was my grandmother."

Her gaze flickered with emotion, but she didn't speak. He told himself Catarina had every reason to hesitate. How many times had he distanced himself, driving her away? It was all in the name of denying this feeling of restless passion that had grown into something much stronger. And yet, despite all the ways he had pushed her away, she was still here. She saw him clearly for all his faults and shortcomings, and still, she was here.

Her eyes were soft, and finally she spoke. "You're not afraid of…?" Catarina gestured to the building around them, all the windows that gave a view of the most pivotal moment of his life.

He raised an eyebrow at her. "I had planned to do this somewhere private."

A hint of a smile twitched at the corners of her mouth, and his heart surged.

"But I am here, down on my knee, in front of anyone who is watching, because my love for you is far stronger and far more important than any fear. I do not want to live without you."

His heart felt as if it was going to burst as she reached for the ring and slipped it on her finger.

"Yes, I will marry you, Massimo." Her voice sang in his body as she brushed her palm over his cheek.

He closed his eyes, soaking in the softness of her touch, the heat of her nearness, the desire that would never go away. And in this beautiful moment, he let himself simply feel all of it. When he looked at her again, he saw a hint of tears in Catarina's eyes, but she was smiling with a kind of joy that made his heart feel as if it were expanding inside his chest. She leaned closer and kissed him with the lightness and hope she had on the first day, in her father's library. This time, he would not squander the opportunity she promised with it.

"I love you, Massimo," she whispered.

It was as if these words reached into his soul, then grew, permeating every part of his being. He could feel the truth that resounded in them, speaking to a truth inside himself. There had been joy and an overwhelming relief when she had agreed to marry him, but these words of love were different. They were everything.

He kissed her the way he had ached to kiss her from the moment he had seen her. The kiss was full of promises and dreams and the satisfaction that they had all the time in the world to explore. It tasted of the future.

Massimo pulled back. "Now will you come up to my flat?"

Her eyes were wild with heat. "Your neighbors will talk."

"Then let's give them something to talk about." Massimo slid one arm under her legs and the other around her body. She laughed as he lifted her and started for the elevator. There would be time to talk about their future later. But for now, it was just the two of them, and there was nothing else on earth he wanted.

EPILOGUE

Catarina looked out at the sparkling fjord and the beach that spread out in front of them, a long, empty stretch of white sand below the green hillside and rocky cliffs. They had hiked down the winding trail from their house to the shore in search of the perfect picnic spot to celebrate their second anniversary. The sun was warm on her skin, and the sky was a bright, cloudless blue that her mother would have loved. The thought of her mother no longer held the sharp pain it had before she met Massimo. The ache of her loss was a larger part of the passage of time in her life, and time had brought her not only great sorrow but also great joy, particularly in the form of the man who now held her hand.

"Here?" he asked, gesturing to their favorite spot, just above the tide line.

Catarina nodded, and Massimo set his pack in the sand. She shook out an enormous beach blanket, and they unloaded an assortment of small containers of food that Signe had prepared for them with strict instructions not to peek, as well as a bottle of wine and one of sparkling water.

When their picnic was neatly arranged, Massimo sat

on the blanket and lifted off his shirt. Catarina couldn't keep her eyes off the movement of his well-honed muscles. His bronze skin glowed in the sun, and she felt a bolt of familiar desire spread through her. Massimo flashed her a wicked smile, as if he could read her thoughts. His hair had gotten a bit longer, and it hung over his forehead with a casualness that still surprised her. He was so different from the man she had met in her father's library. And over the past couple of years, she had felt more truly herself than she ever had.

"I'd like a swim first," she said. "Join me?"

Massimo leaned back on his arms and stretched out his long legs. "Not a chance in this cold. But I'd love to watch."

She stripped off her dress, revealing a new tiny bikini, and she could feel the heat of Massimo's gaze on her.

"Don't take too much time," he added with a roughness in his voice as she headed for the water.

As she crossed the sun-warmed sand, she thought about the first years of their marriage. They had proved better than she had imagined. Massimo had suggested that she could find a role in the family business, but Catarina had decided she wanted to do something that was truly her own. When she told him as much, he had surprised her with how he immediately deferred to whatever she chose. What he wanted in return was something she was willing to give freely: her love. And in that balance, a bond had grown between them, one that would last, regardless of the path she chose. This had been the key to her parents' success in marriage, after all—the fact that they both genuinely had wanted the other to flourish. Massimo had spent every single day of the past two years showing her that he wanted the same for her.

On the topic of a baby, when they'd first gotten married, they had decided to wait. While she had been thrilled with that possibility, she'd also wanted time for the two of them to strengthen their relationship and figure out how to best live their lives together. And after some consideration, Catarina had decided to pursue a career in music education. While the piano remained a private pursuit, she was excited by the idea of spreading her love of music to others.

"I'd like to have our own children after I know myself a little better," she had told him.

"Whatever makes you happy," he had responded, leaning in for another salacious kiss. "I'm enjoying getting to know every part of you, over and over again."

But now she had graduated from the music education program, and things were changing again…

Catarina waded into the sea until the cool water lapped at her waist. Then she dove under, focusing on the weightlessness of her body, the refreshing chill against her hot skin. She swam out into the endless blue of her favorite place on earth, then turned back to shore. Massimo's gaze was still fixed on her. She swam in and crossed the sand as his gaze dropped to her barely covered breasts, then to her slick, wet thighs. Passing up the towel he offered, she instead lowered herself onto him, straddling him, feeling the satisfying hardening against her core. He laughed as she pressed her body against his sun-kissed skin.

"Happy anniversary to me," he whispered in her ear with a deep rumble of humor and lust. "Is there something you're not telling me?"

He took the weight of her breasts in his hands, as if he could already feel the way they would soon start growing fuller.

She bit her lip. "I missed my period a week ago, but I was waiting to be sure."

He paused and pulled back a little. His eyes were filled with the kind of hope he was still learning to show. "Are you feeling okay?"

The corners of her mouth tugged up. "Much better than okay."

His eyes burned with that intense heat she couldn't seem to get enough of. "Now we have something else to celebrate."

He urged her down, against his warm body, and she tasted the salt on his lips, as he kissed her in that way that always made her forget everything else.

"Maybe we should wait until we are back at the house?" she said with a breathless laugh. "What will the gossip magazines say if someone finds us here?"

It still amazed her that they could now laugh at something that used to haunt his life. But love worked the kind of magic that still surprised her every day.

He pressed his lips to her neck. "They will say I am hopelessly in love with my wife, the way they always do these days."

* * * * *

Did you fall head over heels for
Convenient Wife Conditions?
*Then be sure to check out the next installment in
The Carandini Legacy duet, coming soon!
And why not try these other Harlequin stories
from Rebecca Hunter?*

Pure Attraction
Pure Satisfaction

Available now!

Get up to 4 Free Books!

We'll send you 2 free books from each series you try PLUS a free Mystery Gift.

FREE Value Over $25

Both the **Harlequin Presents** and **Harlequin Medical Romance** series feature exciting stories of passion and drama.

YES! Please send me 2 FREE novels from Harlequin Presents or Harlequin Medical Romance and my FREE gift (gift is worth about $10 retail). After receiving them, if I don't wish to receive any more books, I can return the shipping statement marked "cancel." If I don't cancel, I will receive 6 brand-new larger-print novels every month and be billed just $7.19 each in the U.S., or $7.99 each in Canada, or 4 brand-new Harlequin Medical Romance Larger-Print books every month and be billed just $7.19 each in the U.S. or $7.99 each in Canada, a savings of 20% off the cover price. It's quite a bargain! Shipping and handling is just 50¢ per book in the U.S. and $1.25 per book in Canada.* I understand that accepting the 2 free books and gift places me under no obligation to buy anything. I can always return a shipment and cancel at any time. The free books and gift are mine to keep no matter what I decide.

Choose one: ☐ Harlequin Presents Larger-Print (176/376 BPA G36Y)   ☐ Harlequin Medical Romance (171/371 BPA G36Y)   ☐ Or Try Both! (176/376 & 171/371 BPA G36Z)

Name (please print)

Address   Apt. #

City   State/Province   Zip/Postal Code

Email: Please check this box ☐ if you would like to receive newsletters and promotional emails from Harlequin Enterprises ULC and its affiliates. You can unsubscribe anytime.

Mail to the Harlequin Reader Service:
IN U.S.A.: P.O. Box 1341, Buffalo, NY 14240-8531
IN CANADA: P.O. Box 603, Fort Erie, Ontario L2A 5X3

Want to explore our other series or interested in ebooks? Visit www.ReaderService.com or call 1-800-873-8635.

---

*Terms and prices subject to change without notice. Prices do not include sales taxes, which will be charged (if applicable) based on your state or country of residence. Canadian residents will be charged applicable taxes. Offer not valid in Quebec. This offer is limited to one order per household. Books received may not be as shown. Not valid for current subscribers to the Harlequin Presents or Harlequin Medical Romance series. All orders subject to approval. Credit or debit balances in a customer's account(s) may be offset by any other outstanding balance owed by or to the customer. Please allow 4 to 6 weeks for delivery. Offer available while quantities last.

Your Privacy—Your information is being collected by Harlequin Enterprises ULC, operating as Harlequin Reader Service. For a complete summary of the information we collect, how we use this information and to whom it is disclosed, please visit our privacy notice located at https://corporate.harlequin.com/privacy-notice. Notice to California Residents – Under California law, you have specific rights to control and access your data. For more information on these rights and how to exercise them, visit https://corporate.harlequin.com/california-privacy. For additional information for residents of other U.S. states that provide their residents with certain rights with respect to personal data, visit https://corporate.harlequin.com/other-state-residents-privacy-rights/.